CREATING THE KILLING KIND

Sunlight crept between mountain peaks to cast shadows across the glimmering lake. Leaves fell lightly to the earthen floor as branches swayed in the wind that entered with the rising sun. The rippling water brought calmness, while the fortress of trees brought solitude.

I felt the tug on my line and pulled the pole upward and back. As I did this, the line ran away from me. As I reeled, the line tightened; threatening to snap. I lowered the tip of the pole to give it more slack and reeled faster. I'd reel the line in about 5 ft, only to watch it get pulled out another ten. For a solid fifteen minutes I battled this monster. Finally, a long slimy head broke the surface of the water.

This underwater beast appeared to be close to 6 ft in length, with teeth that could shred flesh from bone. The Musky was the biggest fish I'd hooked onto in this lake. A catch of a lifetime, now only a couple of feet from me. I stepped into the lake. My shoes instantly filling with water and soaking my socks, but I didn't care. I wanted to close the distance between me and my trophy fish. I couldn't help but smile at the thought of my father's face when I walked through the front door with this behemoth in my arms.

The Musky thrashed about like a wild bronco, enraged by the hook in its mouth. Now only inches away. I began backing out of the water to pull the fish onto the shore. As the Musky slid onto the dirt and left the water, the fight inside left as well. It stopped thrashing and laid still.

I put the pole down and leaned over the large fish to pull the hook out of its mouth, but it appeared the Musky had swallowed the hook; which meant I'd have to reach deep inside it's throat to pull it out.

I cautiously positioned myself over the fish to prevent it from thrashing about while I went digging for the hook. I considered simply yanking the fishing line but knew it would pull out all of the fish's internals. Although I was a fisherman, I had a certain level of respect for these creatures and ripping out it's insides felt wrong.

Carefully I stuck my hand into the belly of the beast, eyeing the razor-sharp teeth as I felt around for the hook. I held the mouth in a way that prevented the Musky from biting me and with a little effort I was able to unhook the hook. I slowly pulled it out, careful not to snag it on any other internals within the fish.

Once the hook was clear, I let go of the limp fish. It plopped in the dirt and with one last attempt to escape, it threw it's body in an arcing motion. The head of the Musky hit the hook into my arm, causing it to pierce my skin. Lodging deep into the fleshy part of my forearm. The large fish then landed on top of the fishing line. The weight of the fish caused the hook to be pulled down the length of my forearm, leaving a gash worthy of stitches.

I stared at my open arm. The hook still there. I pulled out the hook and watched as blood filled the open wound like water in a bathtub. The most interesting part about the whole ordeal was that I didn't feel a thing. This would be just one more scar added to the many that already riddled my body. Scars that were added without pain.

I was born with Congenital Insensitivity to Pain (CIP) Disease. A genetic disorder where I feel no pain. Quite frankly, I was lucky to make it this far in life. Most children born with the disease don't make it to their teens, because pain is a warning to danger and without the warning, danger is sure to ensue. Imagine no warning as an individual scarfs down a scalding bowl of soup, or cuts themselves unknowingly, or chews through their lip. There's a number of things that can harm an individual if they have no warning signs to the danger.

I took off my shirt and wrapped it tightly around the wound. I looked down at the fish, laying in a muddy puddle beneath my feet; struggling to breath, but still alive. With my, still soaking wet, shoe I nudged the fish back towards the water. It sat still a moment before flapping it's tail and swimming away. I grabbed my pole and began making my way back home, which consisted of cutting through the trees to find the dirt trail that led to the train tracks. From there it was as simple as following the train tracks north to my backyard.

My mother was outside gardening when I walked up, holding my arm that was wrapped in my bloody shirt.

"Lucas Reid!" she shrieked. "What did you do this time?"

I sighed before responding, "Uh... I accidentally hooked myself fishing. No big deal. I promise."

"Lucas, let me see!" she continued with a mixture of anger and worry.

I unraveled the shirt and my mother sat horrified as she saw the fabric cling to my skin from the drying blood. I peeled it away, revealing a deep gash.

"Oh my, we need to get that stitched up. That's deep," she said, holding a hand to her mouth.

She ushered me into my father's old pickup and drove me to the local clinic. Inside, the clinic was surprisingly empty. My mother grabbed me by the shoulders and ushered me up to the small check-in desk, where a plump brunette with Rosy cheeks sat. Her name was Yvonne.

"Hi, Mrs. Reid. What kind of trouble did our young Lucas get into today?" Yvonne asked.

She didn't know my mother and I because we lived in a small town. She knew us because we were regulars. I'm surprised they haven't taught my mother how to do the stitches herself. It would save a lot of time and money on the medical bills. Bills that a door-to-door salesman and a stay at home mother struggled to pay.

6

"This one's not as bad as the bow and arrow incident, but I still think he'll need stitches," my mother replied.

The bow and arrow incident happened with my best friend Mason Mills. Mason bet me his allowance for the week that he could shoot an apple off my head with his bow, something we witnessed on a TV show. Being that I don't feel pain, I took him up on the bet. He missed drastically and landed the arrow in my left shoulder. They had to surgically remove the arrowhead. It took two layers of stitches to fix that injury. My mother's still recovering. She sobbed for weeks, complaining to my father that with this sort of reckless behavior I wasn't going to make it to my twenties. With all my injuries and scars, one might think I wasn't the sharpest tool in the shed, however, it was quite the contrary. I was simply a smart boy that did dumb things.

"Go ahead and take a seat you two," Yvonne gestured to the open seating in the foyer, "Dr. Miller will be out to take you back in just a moment."

We sat and I looked over at my mom who rubbed at her forehead. "I'm sorry I put you through so much trouble, mom," I said with sincerity.

She looked back at me and smiled softly, then she placed a hand on my cheek and kissed my forehead, "You're worth it."

She was a great woman, my mother. She loved me dearly. I felt a pang of guilt in my chest as I was reminded of all the scary situations I put her through. Like a tank and missile are built for war, my mother was built for tolerance. Any other parent would have probably thrown in the towel a long time ago, but not my mom.

A woman with solid gray hair and a smile that would put any grandmothers to shame, stepped out into the foyer and said, "Come on back, Reid family." Dr. Miller was approaching her seventies, yet the only real indicator of her old age was the gray hair. The doctor took great care of herself and better care of her patients. In fact, I visited this woman so much she might as well be one of my grandmothers. She certainly cared for me like one.

Even though it'd only been a month since my last visit, Dr. Miller asked me to kick off my shoes and step up on the scale. The scale read the same as last month: 164 lbs. Noticing my bloody arm, she decided that last month's measurement for my height, 5' 9", would be fine for my chart.

She took us into a small room with a medical bed, a couple of office chairs, a round swivel chair, and a computer that sat on top of a countertop with a sink. She politely asked me to hop up on the bed, which I was already making my way over to. My mother sat in one of the office chairs and fixated her gaze on one of the posters in the room. What came next she couldn't watch.

Dr. Miller pulled a pair of blue latex gloves from a drawer and put them on. Then she pulled out her suture tray and positioned herself next to me on the swivel chair. With her supplies easily accessible, she began.

She draped my arm with a sheet that had a hole in it, so only the thick wound was visible. She skipped the lidocaine, seeing as I would only feel the pressure of the procedure and no pain. Using a syringe of saline, she squirted inside the wound and began cleaning it out. With some gauze, she dabbed at the excess blood that swirled with the saline to create a light red, almost pink color. Once it was clean, she used a scalpel to cut away some of the damaged skin. Then cleaned it again. She took the bloody gauze and tossed the chunks of it into a tin bowl. Finally, she used some forceps, a needle and thread, and sutured up the wound. Leaving a nice line of stitches and a mother that was satisfied with the results.

"Thank you, Dr. Miller. I'm sure we'll be seeing you soon enough," my mother said wearily.

"No problem," she replied to my mother, then turned to me, "Lucas, I know we've had this talk a hundred times, but I need you to take me seriously; for your mother's sake. You are not invincible, even though you can't feel the pain, the injuries are real. Because of your disorder, you've got to take extra care of yourself. Even more so than the average person. I know sometimes it may feel like you're Superman, but even Clark Kent had his weaknesses. Be smart. Be safe. I love having you as a patient, but let's make an effort to reduce the amount of time we see each other in a month. Deal?"

I nodded, "Deal. Thanks doc."

I hopped off the table and began walking out the door, examining my new stitches with a grin. My mother turned to Dr. Miller and mouthed the words, "Thank you."

We sat in silence for the drive home. The stitches, and facing my mother, was the easy part. Now came the part I dreaded most about these situations. When we pulled into the driveway my father was sitting on our front porch smoking a cigarette. The tip of the cigarette began to droop as it burned. Black ash falling from the tip, yet my father didn't seem to mind. He held a stern stare, as if daring me to break eye contact. Nervously, I got out of the truck to face my father.

"Lucas," he said in a calm voice that carried power with each word, "what happened this time?"

I explained to my father about the fishing incident. He didn't yell or hit me. He never did. It was simply the way he said things, as if he was disappointed or couldn't believe I would do such a thing. Each word carrying the weight of a thousand lashes.

After a stone-faced nod that showed little to no emotion, he said, "Hmmm, well accidents happen, but you need to be more careful son. You know your condition is unique and because of it you need to pay better attention. Now go wash up for supper."

I knew better than to try and explain myself any further or come up with excuses, so I simply nodded and said, "Okay, pops."

As I was walking inside, I glanced over and watched as my father put out his cigarette and stood to embrace my mother. He gave her a kiss and she complained, "Howard, you smell like a campfire. I really wish you'd quit that nasty habit."

He chuckled and said, "I'll tell you what, the day our son stops getting stitches is the day I'll put down the cigarettes."

My mother sighed and did the same stressful rub of the head she did in the doctor's office, "So in other words, never?"

After scrubbing my hands thoroughly, I went into my bedroom to find a clean shirt. I'd tossed the bloody one away at the clinic and been shirtless since the lake.

As I sat on my bed, I realized I hadn't changed my wet socks and shoes either. They were now only damp, but far from dry. I pulled them off and stared at my pruned, ghostly looking feet. The air felt nice, but the smell they emitted was pretty awful. I gagged and decided they could use a quick rinse, so I stripped down and plodded back to the bathroom for a quick wash in the shower.

Not more than five minutes later I was back in my room getting dressed. A room that was surprisingly clean for a teenager. My bed was nicely kept with sheets pulled so tight someone could bounce a quarter off of them. They were colored a soft gray. Everything in my room was simple and neat. The wall was painted a light tone blue. No fancy wallpaper or designs. I didn't have junk or clothes spewed about. All my personal items were tucked away in an organized fashion within my drawers and closet. I had a desk in the corner of my room that held a couple of yellow writing pads and a cup full of mostly black ink pens and a couple red. If someone walked into my room, they'd probably be surprised someone actually lived there. I'm sure they would even throw out the words OCD (Obsession-Compulsive Disorder).

My clothing was as simple as my bedroom. I wore mostly jeans, occasionally I'd wear some solid black sweats or plain colored shorts like I planned on wearing for dinner tonight, and a solid colored T-shirt. I pretty much owned a shirt in every color, but not many of my shirts had a design or logo. For tonight I chose a solid orange shirt. I slid it on and made my way to the kitchen. My stomach grumbled with anticipation for whatever my mother was cooking.

The moment I stepped out of my bedroom door I was met by a pleasant smell that I immediately tried to distinguish. What would we be eating tonight? I wondered. I thought I could identify something sweet. Was it the red wine my mother soaked the steaks in? Or something else? I let my nose lead me to the kitchen where I could hear the soft sizzle of something being cooked on the frying pan.

I walked into the kitchen and saw my father setting the table while my mother worked effortlessly on our meal. It was steak that was being seared in the frying pan. I didn't realize how hungry I was until the sweet red wine marinade made its way deep into the depths of my nostrils, carried through the small tufts of smoke produced by the frying pan. I wasn't sure if wine marinade steak was a common meal in other households, but it was a thing in ours; one of many of my mother's signature dishes.

She loved to cook, and she was good at it too. I watched as she stirred a pot of potatoes, then I realized that instead of standing like a fool and enjoying the aromas of the room, I should probably offer to help.

"Anything I can help with?" I asked both parents.

"Yeah," my dad answered first, "You can take Muffin outside to go to the bathroom."

Muffin was our dog. A large American Bulldog with a little bit of Pitbull in her. The result, a dog the size of a small horse with a massive head and stout muscly legs. Her name was Muffin because my father thought the name would soften the way my mother felt about her, make her less intimidating. She had absolutely no resemblance to a muffin. Her fur was white, and she had one solid black ear. Unlike a muffin that was soft and fluffy, her skin clung to her muscular build so tight it looked as though it could tear.

She was currently lounging in her bed, in the corner of the living room, licking her paws. I was a little grossed out by the sound of her licking. It sounded similar to a child reaching the bottom of a slurpy cup.

"Muffin, come on girl," I called to her. Slapping my thighs while smiling strangely, oblivious to the fact that I was doing this.

She looked up but didn't move. I walked over and nudged her with my foot. "Come on girl," I repeated.

She turned on her back, with her legs in the air, and let her tongue loll out. Waiting for me to rub her belly.

"Damn dog," I mumbled, then granted her wish and rubbed her belly.

Outside the sun dipped behind the mountains, casting a colorful glow across the horizon. I stood a moment; transfixed by the red, yellow, and orange colors the lowering sun created. Muffin pulled hard on the leash to chase a nearby squirrel that shimmied up a tree. After three long, annoying barks she abandoned her chase and let me drag her back into the house.

Waiting for me was a steaming plate of juicy steak, fluffy potatoes, and creamy noodles. Waiting for Muffin was a dry bowl of something brown and crunchy, that smelled stale with a hint of chicken. Yet, she scarfed it up like it was a five-star meal.

I sat down and my mother brought me a tall glass of cranberry juice. Then she sat down and sipped at her sweeter, stronger version of the cranberry juice. This was our cozy setting most nights, all three of us sitting down together at the dinner table and discussing our very different days.

My mother always talked about her day first, because my father always asked her first, "Honey, how was your day?" Tonight, was no different.

"Long, this son of ours is going to be the death of me," she responded as if I wasn't sitting right there, but then gave me a wry smile. "I did get a lot done in the garden though, so that was nice." My mother's flower garden had come full bloom and was looking pretty impressive as of late. "After a day spent gardening and at the clinic there wasn't much left to do. What about you dear? How was work?" she asked my father.

"Well, having the overtime is nice, but putting in the work on a Saturday is never fun. I would have much rather been fishing with my boy." He smiled a crooked smile my way as he said this. "Then maybe we could've avoided another doctor's visit. I ended up closing a deal though, so it was good."

My father worked for United Waste Services (U.W.S.). He secured contracts for their garbage pickup, sold dumpsters. That sort of thing. He didn't make a killing, but with the overtime he put in and the deals he closed (he was their number one salesman) we survived.

There was a brief moment of silence before my father said, "What about you, champ? Tell us about your day."

I looked down at my plate, stirring my potatoes as I chewed on a piece of steak. When I'd finished my food, I looked up at my father, "Fishing was good." I said excitedly. "I hooked into a big one." I extended my arms to explain the length of the fish, exaggerating just a little.

"You did?" my father said with sincere curiosity.

"Yeah," I said excitedly. "That's actually how this happened." I lifted my injured arm, that I imagined for anyone else would be throbbing right about now. "I was unhooking the beast when he decided to wriggle and knocked the hook into me, which caused me to drop him and he landed on some loose line which pulled the hook down the length of my arm." I gave a full demonstration with my hands.

"So essentially, you hooked the fish then the fish hooked you?" my father said amused.

I nodded.

"Well isn't that some immediate karma. Glad you're okay though."

There were a few minutes of silence as each of us worked on our meal. By now my steak had cooled and lost some of its juices, so I sipped on the cranberry juice to help it go down.

After another ten to fifteen minutes of small talk all three of us had polished off our meal. Every one of our plates clear, minus some fatty parts of the meat and the left-over juices that hadn't dried up. A true testament to my mother's good cooking.

"Pie anyone?" my mother asked.

My father and I both nodded with our mouths hung open like starved pups. Muffin cocked her head to the side and gave us a look as if to say, 'Pathetic.'

No more than twenty minutes later my mother pulled a steaming, bronze crusted pie from the oven. I could smell the cooked cherries and my mouth began to salivate. I plopped on some whip cream and took a bite too big for my mouth. Whipped cream, cherry, and crust fell to the floor in a delicious heap. My mother gave me a scornful look, my father chuckled, and Muffin scurried over to lick up the mess.

I grinned a mouthful of cherries and we all began to laugh, even my mother. Moments like these made me realize how much I loved my little family, just the three of us; and Muffin. It's too bad nothing lasts forever.

After dessert, we all went our separate ways to do our own thing. My dad to the living room to watch the game, my mother went to take a bath, and I made my way to my bedroom.

In my room I went straight to my dresser drawer to pull out the latest edition. I clicked on the lamp that sat on my nightstand and hopped on top of my bed, not bothering to undress or climb under the sheets. I was too eager to dive into another world.

As I flipped through the pages, I became fully immersed in the fictional town of Smallville, Kansas. Page by page I was drawn deeper and deeper into the story that was being told about an ordinary man who grew up in this small town. There was something about knowing a character's origins, the place where it all began, that made them relatable. I followed along as the main character moved from Smallville to Metropolis, using the name Clark Kent as a secret identity. Changing in phonebooths and emerging as Superman.

<u>**Chapter 3**</u>

Another early morning. A silence so heavy one dared
not to breath. I took a slow step and heard a branch
crack beneath my shoe, lifting the weight of the
silence.

"Shhh!" Mason snapped at me.

I instantly stopped moving and peered around me to
see what stirred. Treetops oscillated in the wind.
Small black ants marched in a row close to my feet,
swerving around fallen obstacles such as leaves and
rocks. Birds fluttered in the rustling leaves of the
trees. Aside from that, the forest remained still.

I crouched next to Mason who'd been waiting in our
usual spot. I was running a little late this morning. On
Sundays my mother liked to cook my father and I a
big breakfast. A breakfast I couldn't resist nor turn
down because my mother woke up early to cook it,
knowing I would be leaving as the sun rose. It
consisted of long, thickly sliced slabs of bacon,
scrambled eggs sprinkled with cheese and bits of the
bacon mixed in the middle. She even went as far as
toasting our bread. The only thing we had to do was
spread on the butter and jelly and pour our choice of
juice. Or in my father's case, a steaming cup of dark
roast. She did all this in an effort to keep us close as a
family.

"You're late," Mason mumbled, fiddling with an arrow.
"I've finally found a GPS tracker small enough to fit

into the tail of the arrow." I watched a small blue light blink, hidden in the feathers.

"Whoa," I mused. "You actually got it to work. This is a game changer. How do we track it?"

Mason pulled out his cellphone and clicked into an app, "Through this app. I created it myself." Mason Mills was as techy as they come. Anything electronic, he could take apart, put back together, rewire, rebuild. You name it. If it involved technology, he knew what he was doing. "Come on, you want to try it out? I spotted a rabbit earlier, but your noisy arrival scared it away." He pointed to the spot he claimed to have saw the rabbit.

"I didn't see a rabbit," I said.

"Yeah of course not, because you scared it away. You nitwit," he said jokingly.

"Shut up and give me the arrow," I joked back.

He handed me the arrow with the blinking light in its tail. I examined it with a close eye before stuffing it into the quiver I had slung over my shoulder.

"Alright, it's active," he said. "So, whenever you're ready."

"I'm ready," I responded.

"Then why did you put the arrow away?" Mason asked confused.

"Because we've got to go find our prey," I stated with a sly grin.

"I told you, the rabbit is just beyond the foliage," Mason continued with the confused look still on his face, pointing to the bushes he claimed a rabbit resided in.

"We're not hunting a rabbit," I said with an even bigger grin.

"We're not?"

"No," I smiled even bigger still.

"Then what are we hunting?" The look of confusion began to turn to a look of concern.

"Boar," my biggest smile yet.

"You're joking?" Mason said worryingly.

"Think about it," I pushed.

"Think about what!?" Mason practically yelled.

"The money! Think about the money we would get for the meat. You know Mr. Simms would pay us fair," I said convincingly.

Mr. Simms was a fifty-year-old man who owned the local butcher shop, Slim Simms: Custom Meats. The ironic part was that Simms was far from slim. He was

by no means fat, but he was wide. He was built like a
small house, short and stout. He had the girth of a
bear with the muscle of a lion. He was the spitting
image of what I would imagine if I thought of a
butcher. Some meathead slapping down a knife to cut
a recently murdered animal, while splaying blood all
over a perfectly white apron.

"Yeah, the money would be nice, but to kill a boar
we're going to have to go into the heart of the forest
and you know what happened to the last teenagers
that attempted going that deep into the unknown." I
was seeing sincere fear on Mason's face as he said
this.

"No, nobody knows," I said honestly.

"Exactly!" he belted out.

"Oh, quit being such a little girl. They probably just ran
away. Wanted out of this boring town full of a bunch
of up-tight people like yourself," I said, half joking.

I continued to walk, not waiting for a response. We'd
never gone deeper than the outskirts of the forest.
The lake was the furthest we'd ventured, which
allowed a view of the town. However, it was rumored
that the wooded area stretched for miles and miles
after the lake. Some people claimed there were more
lakes deeper in the forest. Lakes that would engulf the
one on the fringe, looming dark and mysterious.
Absent of sun from the high growing trees and
surrounding mountains. Others believed a chain of
caverns and caves lead into the mountainside. One

thing was for sure, a large mountain range lay beyond; given away by the mountain peaks lying right above the treeline. Indicating all nature in that direction with no chance of civilization.

Today I was determined to figure out what lay beyond our fishing lake and we had the whole day to do it. One thing we knew for sure was that wild boar resided deep in the forest, it was believed that the whole reason rabbits lived on the outskirts was to avoid the feral pigs that feasted on them deep within.

I didn't bother looking back to see if Mason was following. I knew when it came down to it he'd catch up. Even if he was scared, he'd power through it. He was a team player like that. After about ten steps I heard his crunching footsteps fast approaching.

We always packed water bottles and granola bars because we were usually gone majority of the morning when we went hunting. After about an hour and a half of walking, Mason asked if we could take a break. I granted his request and found a sturdy rock to sit on. I pulled out one of the water bottles and took a long swig before tossing it to Mason. It was a little warm from being stuffed in the small bag I carried with my quiver, but it served its purpose.

While Mason was quenching his thirst, I scanned the area. Looking for signs of a wild boar, and I found some. A few feet from where I sat, in the moist dirt that was only a liquid away from being mud, there was an animal print.

"Look," I said to Mason, pointing at the print.

He studied it carefully, "Could be a deer."

"No," I said with certainty. "It's too short and wide. That's a boar's print. I'd bet my water rations on it." Mason knew better than to take that bet.

"Then I'd say we've gone far enough," Mason said hopefully.

"Mason, did you know wild boar travel in groups?" I asked.

He hesitated a moment, not liking where this was going, "No, I did not."

"A group of boars is called a sounder of swine," I continued, "which makes me believe this was just a straggler that got away from the group. I'm sure he's long gone by now. We need to go further."

Instead of responding, Mason groaned and sipped more water. Then we were on our way. Marching deeper into the forest than we, or anyone else in the town (minus the missing teens and those that searched for them), had gone before. Darkness grew as the number of trees thickened and blocked the warm reassuring sunlight. We did our best to keep a straight line, so we'd be able to find our way back, but after a few patches of trees forced us off our track Mason came up with the genius idea to stick one of the GPS arrows in a tree trunk. As long as we had service, he'd be able to get us back, so far we were in good shape; his phone switching back and forth between two and three bars. I took out one of the few blinking arrows and with ease shot it into the nearest tree.

Sweating profusely from trekking up the mountain, we'd reached an area that looked habitable for boars. There was a small pond, or what I assumed could be their watering hole. Low hanging leaves for shelter, peppered with wild berries. Several trees had roots above the ground that had chunks gnawed on.

"Let's set up here," I said to a breathless Mason.

Between gasps for air, he said, "That works for me."

Mason began gathering severed branches and loose leaves to create some extra cover for us beneath a couple of low hanging trees. I crouched with my bow and arrow at the ready and we waited.

After what felt like hours, but was more like thirty minutes, Mason tapped my shoulder and pointed at a pair of bushes grouped together. The bushes were rustling as if someone, or… something was about to emerge.

I gripped the handle of my bow tighter, my fingers clenching firmly as excitement and anticipation crept through my muscles. I pulled back the bow string, leaving no slack as I readied for the release. The soft blinking light in the arrow's feathers was almost therapeutic, allowing a calmness to settle over me. I focused on my breathing, keeping my eyes dialed in on the rustling bushes, and slowly the world around me dissolved.

It was me and whatever was about to emerge. I could hear it before I could see it. Short heavy breaths intertwined with the sound of sniffing. It was hunting. Using its keen nose for scouting out food, which is why the snout was the first thing I saw break through the leafy wall. A snout that held tusks that looked as though they could tear through flesh as easy as a finger could cut through water. The elongated head with tusks was followed by a girthy body held up by four short legs.

Once I was able to see the whole hog, from the tip of its snout to the wag of its tail, I found the spot I wanted my arrow to land. Before I could even release a full breath, I let go of the bow string.

A deep throated grunt escaped the boar's mouth before it attempted a step forward and fell on its side. It didn't die instantly and sounded like it was in pain so without hesitation I pulled out my knife and ran at it, thrusting the blade into its side in rapid succession. I probably looked like a madman, but I was skilled and with efficiency I ended the boar's suffering.

I almost forgot Mason was there until I heard him sneeze, still hidden.

"Come on, I need your help," I prompted.

He hesitated a moment before stepping out of our hideaway. Once he was next to me, he snapped out

of his trance and began getting the freezer bags
ready. Luckily, he always kept the box in his backpack
because one bag, that we typically used for rabbit
meat, wasn't going to be enough. I did all the knife
work; skinning it, pulling out the insides, and
separating the valuable meat from the meat that
wouldn't sell well.

After we had the meat all packed up, I used some
water to clean the arrowhead I pulled from the boar.
Meanwhile, Mason walked around with his phone in
hand extending it as high up as he could reach;
searching for a signal so we could track back to the
arrow I shot in the tree.

It was pretty comical watching Mason walk around
with his hand held above his head as he stared at his
phone screen. I was waiting for him to walk into a
tree, but something else happened instead.

He disappeared beneath the Earth's surface and all
that was left, where he stood, was a few floating
leaves.

<u>**Chapter 4**</u>

For a moment, I was stunned. My thoughts shattered into a hundred pieces, trying to find their way back together.

"What just happened?" I asked myself as I ran to the spot where Mason disappeared.

Where he'd been walking before he disappeared, there was now a hole. I strained my eyes trying to see into the darkness but couldn't quite make anything out. Then I heard groaning. It didn't sound too far away.

"Mason??" I shouted down the hole.

"Of course, it would be the guy that actually feels pain that would fall down the hole," he said.

He wasn't yelling, so I assumed he was close. I pulled out my phone and shined the light into the hole. In the illumination of my phone's flashlight, I could see jutting rock walls and a rough looking Mason holding his thigh.

"Scraped my thigh pretty bad," he muttered.

Using some of the protruding rocks, I climbed down to Mason. It was only about four or five feet.

"Can you stand?" I asked.

"Yeah, but I don't want to," he said irritably. "You just
had to kill a boar. Now I've fallen in a hole and hurt my
leg. We better get paid well."

"Quit your…" I trailed off mid-sentence.

My phone light scanned over more of an opening.
This wasn't a hole. It was an entrance to a cave.
Damp rocks jutted out to form a hallway of sorts. I
traced my hand along the moist rock as I went deeper
into the cave, letting my phone's flashlight keep the
darkness at bay.

"You just going to leave me here?" I heard Mason cry
out from behind me.

"You can come if you'd like," I said, not playing into
his need for pity. "Or, you can wait while I explore,
and I can come back for you."

I didn't hear a response. Instead, I heard an echo of
footsteps approaching as Mason joined my side.

"My leg is killing me," he complained.

"You seem to be walking fine," I pointed out. He was
keeping steady with my fast pace as we continued
into the unknown. Leaving the safety of the daylight
and surface behind.

We were descending so subtly that if I wasn't using
my phone light we wouldn't have known.

"Where do you think it leads?" Mason asked, with a slight hint of worry in his voice.

"I don't know, but we're going to find out," I said.

The light only cast itself about five feet in front of us, which made it hard to see just how far the rock tunnel stretched. One foot after the other. Minute after minute, we marched further, and I couldn't quite rid my mind of the lingering thought about the missing teens. I wasn't going to mention that to Mason, who was already worried, but in my brain the looming thought sat, burning a tinge more with each step.

After what felt like an eternity, we reached an opening to the tunnel. The walls pulled away, revealing a large cavern. Mason pulled out his phone and clicked on the flashlight. Together, the phones gave us a better view of what laid ahead. The cavern had ledges extending from the surrounding walls. The floor split off going left and right, creating a circular cliff around fairly deep water. The water looked dark and ominous, even with our bright light shining across it.

"Whoa," mumbled Mason.

For a moment we stood in amazement, then I inched closer to the edge of the cliff, peering down. A piece of rock broke away from the side and plopped into the water. It was easily fifteen feet to the surface with no visible way of getting out if one of us fell in. I wondered to myself how deep the water went and what might be waiting in those depths. If anything, I imagined it would be hungry and eager for a meal. These thoughts pulled me away from the edge.

"Alright, I'm ready to head back," I said turning toward Mason.

"Lucas," he practically whispered. He looked frozen.

"What?" I whispered back, unaware of why we were whispering.

"Did you hear that?" he said even quieter than before.

"Hear what?" I said confused.

"I think something's in here with us."

Instead of responding I clicked off my light. Mason did the same. A darkness that belonged to the dead of night took over us. I couldn't see the outline or shape of anything; only a mass of black. There was no change from opening my eyes to staring at the back of my eyelids. I leaned my head to the side as if perking up my ears would help my hearing. For a few seconds we sat and listened. Then I heard it.

It sounded like footsteps plodding against the dirt and rock mixed floor. Heavy and big sounding footsteps. I could tell they were still a way away by the soft echo they produced through the cavern's tunnel entryway. I was grateful for the natural design of the cave, with its long tunnel into the great opening where we stood, it took the sound and reverberated it off the jagged walls, giving us forewarning of a visitor. Now the question was, what to do about it?

"Do we hide and attack whatever it is?" Mason whispered with a weak voice.

"Uh… I don't think that would pan out too well for us, Mase. We've got a circle here, let's use that to our advantage to run away from this thing because I'm guessing it's an animal and most animals you meet in caves aren't friendly. Plus, those footsteps sound like they belong to Sasquatch and I'm not attacking Sasquatch," my whispering fluctuated and then I realized that if we could hear footsteps, this thing could probably hear our whispers; forewarning it of unwanted guests.

The sound of the footsteps quickened. Growing closer. I tensed in preparation. My heart joined pace with the quickening footsteps. Then, right as we were preparing to run… the footsteps stopped.

It was like existing in nothingness. For no more than a split second, sound ceased, and darkness was engulfing us. I fiddled with my phone, trying to get the screen unlocked to get the flashlight back on. When I finally got the flashlight turned back on, I flashed the light back down the way we came.

Silhouetting the mouth of the tunnel we'd just come out of, was a bear. It was a mangy looking thing with matted fur. It was hard to distinguish the color of the fur under the phone's light, but by the size of it, it appeared to be a black bear. A lot smaller than its cousin, the grizzly and for that I was grateful.

It stood on its hind legs and cocked its head at us before dropping back on all fours and charging. I split off to the right and Mason took off to the left. His light was off now, but mine danced around wildly as I ran. Throwing shadows off the cave walls. The bear's growling and pounding paws echoed throughout the cavern so it was hard to figure out if it was chasing me or Mason. It's large shadow behind another, smaller, shadow on the far wall with both shadows running made it hard to figure out which of us was the smaller shadow.

I glanced over my shoulder and caught my other shoulder on a protruding rock, I didn't feel any pain but it launched me into a spin that I struggled to come out of. I dropped my phone and was slightly disoriented. I stepped forward and felt the air of nothing beneath my foot. Uh-oh. Wrong way. I fell, backwards and grasped at dirt and gravel to pull myself away from the edge.

I searched frantically for my phone. It must have landed in a way that covered up the flashlight because I wasn't seeing anything.

"Plop."

Something bigger than a rock had plunged into the water.

"Mason!?" I shouted with undeniable worry in my voice.

A light clicked on from the opposite end of the cavern.

"I'm alright, how are you?!" He shouted back.

Our conversation echoed throughout the cavern, joined by growls and moans carried across the water. By Mason flashing his light towards me, I was able to find my phone. We both shined our light down in the water, searching for our attacker.

Closer to Mason than me, the bear bobbed up and down. Pawing at the slick rock wall. Going up a foot, then falling like a bag of bricks beneath the water. We watched this routine for a few minutes before realizing we should probably get out of there. I took pity on the bear though, it moaned and struggled to climb the wall. After all, we impeded on its home and now it was the one stuck in the water. But what could I do? Help it out? It'd tear us to shreds. So, we left. Hoping it would figure a way out. However, I couldn't rid myself of the gut-wrenching guilt that festered in my stomach.

"Let's go hunt boar, rabbits aren't scary enough," mocked Mason with a mixture of different hand gestures.

"That's the most excitement you've had in a year," I said with a big grin.

It was easy to smile and joke now we were out of the cavern and away from Yogi Bear's cousin. Mason had his phone out and was using his app to get us back to the arrow I'd shot into the tree. Thank the heavens for GPS tracking.

As we walked a breeze kicked up the stench that was a result of two scared, teenage boys. My shirt was damp with sweat as was the rest of my body. It was a combination of fear sweat and heat sweat. I took my forearm and used it to wipe some of the sweat from my forehead. It returned with a large dirt mark. I was going to need a shower.

We were both exhausted as we trekked back. All I could think about was splashing my face with cold water and collapsing in front of a fan. The idea of ice cubes in a cold glass of water waiting for me at home made me pick up pace. Even with the shade of the everlasting trees, I could not cool down. Sweat continued to pool underneath my pits. Step after step, I began to think this was a bad idea after all. Mason believed it was a bad idea from the start.

Finally, after much zigzagging and hiking through rough terrain, we'd reached the arrow and it's blue blinking light. Mason gripped it and pulled, but the arrowhead stayed buried in the trunk of the tree. He tried again. This time it moved a little. Before he could attempt it a third time, I stepped up and with one fluid motion, yanked the arrow from the tree. I tossed it to him and kept walking.

"I loosened it," he shouted at me.

"I know you did," I shouted back.

When we returned to my house, we parted ways, with the intention of linking back up to hit the town after a nice long nap and shower. Not necessarily in that order and before all of that I needed to get the boar meat stored nicely in the freezer so it would be ready to sell to Mr. Simms. We didn't go through all of that for nothing. Today was payday.

Chapter 5

The first thing I did when I entered the house was make myself my desired glass of water with extra ice. The first sip quickly turned to a gulp that turned equally as fast to a chug. The warm water in our backpacks just wasn't the same. There was something about the way ice cold water froze my insides and numbed my brain. It was refreshing.

Cooled down from the ice-cold water, I opted for a warm shower. The drizzling water put me in a state of bliss that bordered sleepy and like a magnet, I was pulled to my bed. I fell like a chopped tree and before my head hit the pillow, not figuratively speaking, literally, before my head hit the pillow, I was asleep.

After an hour or more of sawing logs, I woke up feeling like a new person. I had all kinds of newfound energy. I threw on some jeans and a bright red T-shirt. That was about as flashy as it got for me. Then I called up Mason.

He answered with a hoarse voice, "Hel… Hello."

"You still sleeping?" I asked, feeling completely rejuvenated.

"I was, butthead," he spat back.

I told him to meet me at my house to help with all the meat. He lived less than five minutes away by bike. While I waited for him to come over, I went to the freezer and began packing up all of the meat; attaching dollar signs to every slab of the boar I threw in the bag. I couldn't help but grin. A rabbit split between two of us barely bought a new comic book. This large scale of meat could buy us a new collection of comic books as well as leave some left over change for the piggy bank. At least that was the hope.

Backpacks full, I stood in my driveway with my vision struggling against the blaring sun to see Mason. Once a little cloud coverage blocked out the sunlight, I was able to see him rolling up the street. I would say pedaling, however, he'd somehow managed to install a tablet that connected to the chain of his bike and propelled it by the push of a button. The braking system was set up the same way. Mason's bike was therefore no more than a means for transportation, considering he'd removed all possibilities for any exercise. In other words, he didn't pedal to get that thing moving. Me on the other hand, I guess I was a little bit old school; I still used old-fashioned pedaling as the way of propelling my bicycle. A walk to town was doable, but unlike going to the lake, it was far from enjoyable. On the bikes we made it there in no time. Mason before me, because in this John Henry story the machine beat the man.

Mr. Simms's place was an old standalone building. It was built up using red brick that had faded so much it was on the brink of being brown. The updated sign that read, Slim Simms: Custom Meats, made it seem like the antique look was intentional. His logo, pasted on the new sign, was a pig's head with a fat bladed axe behind it.

We locked our bikes to a lamp post right outside the butcher's shop. Mason double and triple checked the lock, making sure no one would be able to steal his bike. I debated even locking my bike up.

Mr. Simms was outside when we walked up. He was leaning against the wall right outside his door and had a bag full of sunflower seeds that he was cracking open in his mouth and littering across the pavement.

"Hello boys," he said in a friendly tone. "More rabbit meat for me today?"

"Not today," I answered before Mason.

He looked confused for a moment and eyed our backpacks, "No?"

"Nope, Lucas killed a boar!" Mason blurted out with excitement.

"You don't say?" Mr. Simms said in disbelief. "Well follow me inside. We'll weigh it and see what we can pay you boys." He cracked one last seed and spit it at his feet before turning and heading into his shop.

I stared at the mess of seeds on the ground wondering if he had any intention of sweeping them up or not, then shrugged away the thought and caught up to Mason and Mr. Simms inside.

Unlike the outside brick, the inside of the shop was recently updated and very modern looking. There were large glass cases covering the far wall with an assortment of meat. Each with a label that identified the meat. There wasn't much else in the front of the store aside from a counter with a cash register. Mr. Simms ushered us through plastic slats to the back where there was a large steel table, he used for slicing and dicing the meat. On that same table sat a fairly big scale.

We produced the meat from our backpack and handed it over to Mr. Simms. He weighed it one bag at a time. The meat totaled around a hundred pounds and Mr. Simms offered $2.50 a lb. which meant a total of $250 so $125 for Mason and $125 for me.

"This was a good kill boys. You did a good job preserving all the meat too. I should have no problem selling this. Say, next week do you think you could bring me a bear?" Mr. Simms had a serious look on his face as he asked this and handed over our cash.

Mason and I exchanged looks of disbelief before Mr. Simms said, "I'm only kidding. Don't go hunting no bears. I'd hate to have you end up like those teens. Both your parents would have my head."

We wrapped up with Mr. Simms and he followed us back out to resume his post on the corner with his sunflower seeds, shouting after us, "Always a pleasure doing business with you boys. Have a good one."

We waved goodbye and proceeded deeper into town for a place to spend some of our hard-earned cash.

As we rolled along on our bikes, we passed a variation of stores and restaurants. Our first stop after the butcher's, we decided, would be the supermarket. We figured since we now had some cash in our pockets that we'd start by snagging some snacks. We often substituted our lunchtime meal with chips and soda. Luckily, we were active enough to keep the extra lbs at bay. It didn't stop our sodium intake from being through the roof though.

The local supermarket was named, Nature's Market. They sold a lot of organic, healthy foods mostly, but they also had an aisle dedicated to the unhealthy snacks we liked.

We walked down the aisle of snacks scouting out our usual. My usual was a bag of pretzels, package of Skittles, and a Coke. Mason went with Doritos, Sour Patch Kids, and a Dr. Pepper.

On our way to the cashier we cut through the produce section. I brushed my hand across a pile of watermelons as I peered across a sea of fruits and vegetables. Then I saw her.

She was sorting through a stack of apples, so at first all I could see was her side profile. She wasn't very tall, but she was lean. She wore a tight dress that complimented her curves and cut off above the knees to display a stunning pair of legs that had obviously been used for running over the years. Her hair was pulled into a ponytail except for a strand that fell over her cheek.

She must have felt me staring because she turned to look at us, brushing the strand of hair behind her ear. She gave a polite smile that revealed straight white teeth below plump, juicy looking lips; strategically placed on the face of an angel. She was unnaturally beautiful and, in that moment, I believed in love at first sight.

Mason nudged me with an elbow, "You're being awkward. Roll your tongue back into your mouth and pick up your jaw."

"Who is that?" I mumbled softly, finally pulling my gaze away.

"Maybe she's our new teacher?" Mason suggested with a cheesy grin.

Our current teacher, Mr. Stein, had a heart attack recently. He was in full recovery, however, his wife asked him not to return to teaching. She thought it was partially the cause of his heart attack, too much stress. On top of that, they decided to relocate. Move out of our small town and all its gossip. With school starting not too long ago, the administration was in a rush to find a replacement so Mason could be right. It was possible that this beauty in the produce aisle was our new teacher.

I watched her examine a few more apples in my peripherals, carefully choosing those that were the ripest in the bunch.

Pulled from my trance, I followed Mason to the checkout stand where we were greeted by Gary Sanders. Gary was a retired old man who didn't want to sit at home and do nothing for his remaining years, so instead of doing that he got a job at Nature's Market.

"You boys ever think about visiting the produce section?" Gary said with a friendly smile as he scanned our items.

Mason was the first to answer, "We just did, had to cut through there to get here."

We may be stopping by for some produce sooner than you think, I thought to myself remembering the gorgeous woman we'd recently encountered there.

Gary chuckled; this wasn't the first time he'd rang us out with a couple bags of junk food. Then he said, "You boys better enjoy getting away with it now. Once you're my age, every Cheeto you eat is a pound you gain."

As we walked to our next destination for spending our money, we snacked. I'd found some repetition with popping a pretzel in my mouth and taking a swig of the Coke. The two paired perfectly. Mason devoured his Sour Patch Kids with ease as he shoved handful after handful into his mouth. I couldn't help but think how simple life was in that moment.

The next shop we stopped at was the local bookstore. It was called Page Turners. Funny enough, the owner's last name was Turner. A clever play on words. I always hoped he'd marry a woman named Paige, because that would just be perfect. However, Lance Turner didn't really seem like the type to get married. He was a tall slender man who barely made it to work without being startled by his own shadow.

Although we loved the whole atmosphere of the bookstore, we didn't go to Page Turners for the novels or the mediocre coffee. The section we went for was strategically placed in the back of the place.

It was its own little corner, easy to tell where the beginning was because of the two cardboard cutouts that greeted us upon arrival. One of the cutouts was Thor bringing down a string of lightning with his hammer. The other cutout was the Hulk punching a crater size hole in the cement.

I slightly disliked the fact that Lance Turner opted for Marvel displays over DC, but to each their own. Mason had a good way of being unbiased. His favorite comic book characters were Batman who was a DC character and Ironman who was part of Marvel. He loved the fact that neither had actual powers, but both used their intelligence, and money, to create gadgets that made them powerful. I think we all idealize fictional characters we wish we could become; it gives us hope and aspiration. The same way a dysfunctional or imperfect novel character is easy to like and relate to, they make us feel better about our own imperfections; better about being human and we see something in these characters we see in ourselves.

While Mason went digging through the paper-thin stacks of Ironman comic books, I thumbed a few twenty-dollar bills and headed towards the hardbound books. There was one specifically I'd been eyeing for the day I came across some money.

The book had a solid brown, leather cover with a black Superman logo and read:

Life of the Man of Steel.

Monday morning, Mason and I cut across the baseball field to the back of the school where our lockers were located. As we got closer to the building, I noticed small clouds of smoke rising from behind the dugout.

There was a group of seniors puffing one of those trendy vape pens, some form of an electronic cigarette; they were pretty commonplace now.

There were four of them. Three boys and a girl. The girl was Tenzie Zhou. Her family owned a Chinese restaurant in town. It was authentic and delicious. My family went there often. She was a pretty girl who got mixed up with the wrong crowd and with the wrong guy.

Mark Woods, or to his friends "Woody," was Tenzie's boyfriend. A large football player who truly believed he ran the school with his two goons Todd and Scott, the dinguses trying to blow "O's" in the air next to him.

Tenzie was the first to notice us walking by and teased, "Hello boys, care for a smoke?" She smiled a playful smile that showcased how pretty she was.

"Those losers don't smoke," chuckled either Scott or Todd. It was easy to get the two mixed up.

Woody stood and walked over to us with one of the vape pens in his hand. He blew a puff of smoke and pushed the vape pen in front of our faces, "Take a hit, boys."

I expected to smell a burning scent, but instead the smoke smelled sweet; like a cupcake. It was actually pleasant, which made "taking a hit" sound somewhat appealing.

"We're good," I said deciding I wasn't going to smoke for Woody's benefit.

Woody stepped closer, towering over us like a father to his child. Amazing what a few years could do for someone's size.

"I'm not asking you," he said with a stone-cold face.

Mason and I didn't respond. Instead, we continued walking toward the school. I was closest to Woody, so he reached out and grabbed my backpack to pull me back, but in a fluid motion I wiggled out of it and yanked it from his hand.

He stood a moment clenching the fist that failed to snag my bag. His face reddened and I stood face-to-face with him to see what he'd do next.

When he did nothing I smiled and said, "That's what I thought."

Without hesitation he swung one of his colossal fists at my face. Anticipating this move I quickly side stepped. Woody's momentum kept him moving forward and he almost fell over. This angered him even more so he took a swing with his left hand this time, the fist that was clutching his vape pen.

The second punch was closer, skimming my cheek, but he still missed and because of that he was now enraged. He charged at me like a linebacker gunning for the quarterback. I juked to my right with a quick step then dropped down on my knee, using his forward momentum I flipped him on his back.

He laid there like an injured animal, clutching his chest, and gasping for air. The vape pen had fallen from his grasp and laid on the ground. I was tempted to steal it but thought better of it. His two goons ran to his side, his girlfriend stayed put and continued to smoke, and Mason and I got out of there.

Mason knew better than to ask where I'd learned to fight like that. He already knew. I'd been fighting since before the first grade. Always running to aid someone in trouble. Nine times out ten that someone was Mason due to some unintentional smart remark. Plus, it's fun to fight when you don't feel pain.

As we approached the double doors to our school my eyes fell upon a stunning woman in a tight dress that showed off her fit legs. She had a ponytail pulled tight with one loose strand and she stood staring right at us. I wondered if she'd witnessed the whole thing. Without any form of expression, she whipped around and disappeared into the school.

That same, gorgeous woman, from the grocery store introduced herself as Vera Bristol.

She stood in front of the class with all her beauty and stated, "I am your new teacher on a temporary basis for now. I'm not sure how long I'll stay. Could be a few months. A year. A few years. Who knows, but as long as I am here, we are going to make the most of our time together. Deal?"

A few students in the class mumbled a poorly stated, "Deal."

A lot of the male students sat up in their chairs as Ms. Bristol spoke, while the girls looked distasteful at her.

Ms. Bristol looked left to right, analyzing her new class. It was as if she was gauging each student, trying to read them. When her eyes met mine, I felt as though she was peering into my soul. Lifting the curtain of thought that shielded my private life and revealing all my secrets. It was the way she looked at me. The twinkle in her eyes holding knowledge and understanding. It was as if she knew secrets about myself that I didn't even know.

She turned and walked up to the whiteboard, pulled the lid off a marker and announced, "I'm going to write a question on the board. Whoever answers correctly will receive a prize. Ready?"

A lot of the class nodded in agreement and craned their neck to see what she was now writing on the board.

'The Theory of...' was all she had written when she turned back to the class, stating, "Everyone take their phone out and put it face down on your desk. There will be no Googling the answer."

There wasn't a student in the room who didn't have a personal cellphone sitting in front of them. Once Ms. Bristol was satisfied that there would be no way of cheating, she finished writing, '...Merton: Strain Theory.'

"Can anyone tell me what Strain Theory is?" she said in a loud voice as she looked intently at each student.

I glanced over the faces of all my classmates. Every one of them had the look of gears grinding, minds searching, but no answers being found. Surely, I couldn't be the only one who knew what Strain Theory was, I thought to myself. I fought the urge to sit in silence and forced my hand up.

It took a moment for Ms. Bristol to see my raised hand.

She pointed at me, "Ready to take a stab? What's your name?"

I nodded and said, "My name's Lucas."

"Alright, Lucas. Impress me. What is Strain Theory?"

I swallowed a little before speaking, intimidated by her beauty, "Well..." I looked at all my classmates who stared back at me with curious looks on their faces. I caught a glimpse of Mason who looked as curious as the rest of them. "Strain Theory is a criminology theory that explains criminal behavior as a result of unrealistic goals put on individuals by society. Goals such as being financially comfortable without providing the means for people to achieve such goals. A drug dealer is a great example of Strain Theory. Just look at Walter White in Breaking Bad. He was expected to financially support a family while handling medical bills for his lung cancer, society provided him no way out but expected him to pay for his treatment on a teacher's salary therefore he had to resort to selling drugs."

At the Breaking Bad example, the class began a low chorus of chuckles. Ms. Bristol, however, held a curious stare without so much as a crooked smile.

Then her face softened, and she forced her lips upright, "Very impressive, Lucas." She walked to her desk and dug a Snickers out of one of the drawers. In a smooth motion she lobbed it to me without even looking. I caught it with ease and immediately tore back the wrapper to sink my teeth into delicious peanuts and caramel buried beneath rich chocolate.

In an elegant fashion she sat in a chair with her hands in her lap and asked, "Now tell me, Lucas. How come you're the only one in this class who knows what Strain Theory is?"

Her eyes were fierce as they bore down on me. They made me feel as if she was judging me, which I don't know why because what she was asking was a fair question. How did I know what Strain Theory was and how come my class didn't? Even Mason. I've always thought he was the smarter of us two.

After searching the cobwebbed depths of my mind and finding nothing, I responded honestly, "I don't know. I read a lot of psychology and sociology books and articles in my free time as well as listen to audiobooks of various genres. Maybe I picked it up subconsciously in one of those…"

She considered my response and then seemed pleased enough to move on. Ms. Bristol covered an array of topics throughout the remainder of the class, yet she always found a way to correlate each new topic she covered; so, it never seemed like she was going on a tangent. It was easy to see Ms. Bristol was an intelligent woman. Her vocabulary was like none I'd ever heard, but she had a way of dummying things down so we could understand. It made me wonder what a woman like her was doing in a place like this.

After class I expected a run in with Woody and his gang. Back for revenge. It wasn't that I was afraid they'd retaliate; I knew they would. I just wasn't in the mood for it at this particular moment. It'd been an eventful few days and I was hoping for some normalcy for a bit.

The rest of the day went down smoothly. No run in with Woody and nothing out of the norm. Even basketball practice after school was normal. No extra sprints or boring drills. We simply scrimmaged and practiced foul shots; my ideal practice. I got a decent workout and headed home for the night. Eager to shower, relax, and read my new book.

When I got home, however, my plans for an easy-going night were brought to an end when I noticed a stranger's car lurking in the shadows of our driveway. I was hesitant to head inside. My parents rarely had guests over and if they did it was on the weekend. Never on a school night. Unless, it was someone Mason and I had irritated or done something to. In other words, a stranger's car in the driveway usually meant I was in trouble.

With reluctancy, I made my way inside. The house was dark except for the dining room light. It appeared we were having a dinner guest.

<u>**Chapter 7**</u>

Ms. Bristol sat in one of our dining room chairs wearing the same flattering dress from earlier in class. The only difference with her appearance was her hair, now down and flowing past her shoulders. She looked more relaxed this way. I had a hard time believing Ms. Bristol had always been a teacher. Something about her current image didn't fit, but I couldn't quite figure out what.

I could smell meatballs cooking in my mother's famous spaghetti sauce. I was always hungry after practice, but the thought of slurping noodles in front of Ms. Bristol made my stomach knot. Maybe it was her beauty, maybe it was her intellect, maybe it was something else entirely; whatever it was, I cared what this woman thought of me. Which is why I suddenly became aware of my own bodily odors and yearned for a shower.

Ms. Bristol was facing into the kitchen talking to my mother. I couldn't see my father, but I assumed he was in there with them, so before any of them could see or hear me, I snuck upstairs for a quick shower.

Fifteen minutes later with a couple light squirts of cologne, I joined my parents and Ms. Bristol for dinner. After no more than five minutes of sitting there my father sniffed the air then turned to me with a cheesy grin.

"Are you wearing cologne, son?" he asked.

I could feel my cheeks flush from embarrassment. In the corner of my eye I glanced at Ms. Bristol to see if she'd noticed my father's comment. She definitely had. She was chuckling softly.

Not knowing what to say, I responded with, "Oh, yeah. Basketball practice." As if that was enough of an explanation.

With all of us now at the table my mother began dishing up large portions of her spaghetti and meatballs. Followed by her garlic cheese bread. Extra garlicky for my benefit.

Ms. Bristol waited until we'd gotten through most of our meal, inserting an occasional compliment to my mother's cooking, before telling us why she'd stopped by.

"Today in class, Lucas knew the answer to a question none of his classmates knew. It was very impressive," she began.

My father sat up a little, beaming with pride for his son. My mother's smile widened.

Ms. Bristol let that sink in a little before going on, "It made me curious about Lucas, so I pulled his files. A lot of his teachers had not just good, but great things to say about him." She turned to me, "You've impressed a lot of people with your intellect over the years."

Things have always seemed to come easy for me, but I hated math and science growing up, so I never considered myself smart… Smart people enjoyed those kinds of subjects, right?

I didn't say anything, but gave a toothless smile; so, she continued, "I'm not actually a teacher. Well I am, but I'm more than that. I'm sort of a recruiter. I work for the U.S. government. Every few years I'm tasked with a new location. Usually smaller towns, but sometimes cities."

She paused and watched all three of us to see if we were following along. When she was certain that we were, she went on, "There's a program the government has that not many people know about. It's called S.I.C., The 'Sick' program."

"The sick program?" I asked, stifling a chuckle.

She didn't so much as bat an eyelash, "Yes, S.I.C. Skilled Individuals' Community. A place where Individuals from a variety of different ages who are above average intelligence and display impressive physical abilities can reside to push one another. A place where elite students, such as yourself, can live and learn together."

My mother had a concerned look on her face and asked, "Like a school? That he lives at?"

"Kind of," Ms. Bristol responded. "But it's more than a school. It's a community of intellectual people and powerful connections that will give Lucas a head start on a career, on life really."

"Sounds expensive," my father grunted.

Ready for such a response, Ms. Bristol said, "Because it's a government program there's government funding you can apply for. It's the opportunity of a lifetime for Lucas."

My father still didn't look convinced, neither did my mother as my father said, "And you've picked Lucas off of one interaction with him in class?"

Ms. Bristol sighed, "No, not just that. Lucas was very impressive in class today, but my reason for choosing him as a candidate for the S.I.C. program is more than him knowing what Strain Theory is. I've observed Lucas throughout the halls and the way he carries himself in comparison to his peers. It's… it's very mature. He has a professionalism about him in public and that sort of characteristic is exactly what our U.S. government is looking for."

I started thinking back over the day and something popped into my head. Ms. Bristol mentioned that the program was for students with 'impressive physical abilities.' She was considering me because of my fighting skills, I thought to myself. She wasn't going to tell my parents that though. Which made me grateful. I didn't really feel like explaining myself, but that's the only thing that made sense.

"I'm not saying that he's in the program just yet. However, I think my instincts are right about him and I wanted to make you both aware so you can start thinking about it. Because if he is selected, he'll be moved away immediately to start."

"Moved away?" My mother's worries were starting to unfold.

"Yes," was all she said.

"To where?" I could almost hear a subtle waver in my mother's voice.

"That I can't say. For safety reasons of those in the community." Another short and oversimplified answer.

"So…" my father joined in, "Are we going to be able to see him?"

Ms. Bristol looked down and away from my parents, not a very comforting response.

"So, no?" my father said, before a verbal reply came.

"I'm sure we could arrange for him to return home for a holiday or two. Again, let's not get ahead of ourselves. Tonight's visit was to simply make you aware of the program and what it has to offer. Let's focus more on that," she said.

"Okay," my father said, playing along. "Tell us more about this 'sick' community."

It sounded funny the way he said it. Like I was being sent to a place for ill or diseased individuals. Quarantined from the rest of the world. When put that way, it didn't sound like a place I wanted to be. I enjoyed my life as is. I loved my parents. I had good friends. A best friend. I didn't need or want things to change.

Ms. Bristol's face brightened at the request to elaborate on S.I.C. She straightened up even more, which I didn't think possible and said, "The grounds at S.I.C. are breathtaking. Similar to an old-fashioned college campus. Every inch and architectural design on the grounds was created to stimulate and uplift the mood of individuals living there. We aim to keep our residents happy and in an effective mood to learn. The government has invested millions into this program. That's how much they believe in it."

My parents nodded but showed little expression, so it was hard to tell what they were thinking.

With no comments yet, she continued, "A lot of parents worry about their child being well fed. At S.I.C. the food is cooked with nutrition in mind. Healthy, well fed minds produce the best results, so we've brought in a team of nutritionists and highly sought-after chefs to provide the best meal plan for our residents. Your child."

Nice touch on the end, '*your child*.' I found it interesting she kept calling them 'residents' now instead of students.

Before she could go any further my mother interjected, "I'm sorry to interrupt, but I think we've wasted your evening."

Ms. Bristol looked puzzled, "How so, Mrs. Reid?"

Now my mother straightened, "Lucas has a medical conditional. A condition he'll have all his life. It's important that I stay close and that I'm able to see him because of this condition."

Ms. Bristol didn't waste any time in responding, "Are you talking about his Congenital Insensitivity to Pain?"

My mother looked surprised and nodded. It appeared someone had done their homework.

Ms. Bristol leaned forward, "Mrs. Reid, I read about Lucas's condition. It was mentioned in quite a few of his school files. Especially the ones covering his earlier years. Let me assure you, he will be in good hands. The best hands. Part of the funding for this program goes to bringing in the best doctors America has to offer."

Usually at this stage in the evening, when having a dinner guest, my mother would offer some dessert. Her go to dessert was chocolate chip cookies. She had the timing perfect. Putting them on a low heat to be ready to serve roughly fifteen minutes after dinner. When it was an unexpected dinner guest though she went with a simple strawberry cake that consisted of Graham crackers, whipped cream, and of course strawberries. Tonight, however, she made no attempt to serve dessert. The main indicator on how the visit was going.

Although I was flattered Ms. Bristol was considering me for this program. I was happy my parents weren't being easily persuaded.

"If Lucas is selected," Ms. Bristol said, smiling in my direction. For a while I thought they'd forgotten I was in the room. "He'll be very well taken care of. We wish nothing but the best for our residents." There it was again, 'residents.' Something about being referred to as a 'resident' as opposed to a student felt off. "Plus, he'll be linked with some of the most influential people in the world. He'll have a shot at a great career."

My father, opposite of the women, leaned back when he spoke, "A career in what? And who are these 'influential people' you're talking about?"

It was a pretty vague explanation. Filled with lots of calculated selling points.

Ms. Bristol sat for a moment, possibly debating with herself whether or not she should drop a name or go deeper into depth with the program. She probably didn't want to reveal too much before I was selected. It all seemed so secretive and I wasn't quite sure how to feel about that.

"A career in whatever he wants really. We have graduates who go into science. Some big-time politicians. Professors at big universities. Lawyers. Doctors. You name it. We've probably had a graduate do it. The sky is the limit at S.I.C. As I mentioned earlier, for security purposes I can't give you any names of the influencers. I'm sure you understand. I can say, that I'm almost certain you've heard of these people though."

I couldn't tell by the way my father leaned back in his chair how he felt about Ms. Bristol's response and not much else was said as the evening began to wrap up. I was eager for the conversation to be over and our guest to leave because it meant I'd be able to head to my room and get lost in my book.

My father stood up and walked Ms. Bristol to the door, where he flipped on the porch lights and told her to have a good evening. She bid the same to my father and included my mother as well. Then she turned to me and with her warm smile fading said, "Lucas, the S.I.C. program isn't something I want mentioned to other students. Students knowing about the program skews the results. Like a child displaying good behavior because the child knows the parents are watching. I want to observe other students without them putting on a show. You understand?"

I nodded and said, "Have a goodnight, Ms. Bristol. I'll see you in class tomorrow."

At my comment, her warm smile returned, and she climbed into her car to drive away. Leaving my family and I to stew in our thoughts.

Chapter 8

Refusing to change our routine Mason and I cut across the baseball field, where I expected to find our older friends vaping. Instead, we found their usual hangout spot empty. Maybe today was going to be a good day after all. I'd been stewing about Ms. Bristol's visit all night. Debating whether or not I should tell Mason. Ultimately deciding against it until it was actually a thing to consider.

As we entered the school, the halls had been decorated to display banners with the school's colors and read: GOOD LUCK SPARTANS! Some other banners read: Go. Fight. Win. A whole cliché of school pride for today's game.

As requested by our coach, I wore a button up shirt and tie. Most of the other players hated dressing up. I was different. I was the anomaly. I enjoyed being dressed in a professional manner. Maybe that was what Ms. Bristol was talking about last night.

As I was grabbing some books from my locker, Hayley Stewart a girl I used to have a crush on years ago, touched my shoulder. We rarely talked or saw each other anymore, which is part of the reason I think my crush for her faded; but as I turned around, I couldn't help but notice how pretty she'd become. A flood of emotions came rushing back in as she smiled at me, this made me think I should consider pursuing her again. A brief thought was all.

"Good luck on today's game. I know you'll do great," she said, giving me another quick smile and looking away.

"Thanks," I responded to the back of her as she walked down the hall. I couldn't help but think that me being dressed like I was attending a wedding was the reason she'd approached me. Some girls liked a man who could clean up. Or, maybe she was just being nice. Probably the latter.

In class with Ms. Bristol she acted completely normal. Like last night's visit to my house to tell me about some secret government program never happened. Even though I didn't plan on telling anyone about the visit, I don't think they'd believe me if I did. I ran through the whole scenario in my head and it sounded crazy.

Class carried on as normal. Nothing out of the ordinary. As my mind typically did on game days, it wandered to thoughts of how the game would play out. I was lost in one of those thoughts when the bell rang and Ms. Bristol excused everyone, but turned to me, "Lucas, a word."

Mason looked at me with raised eyebrows. "I'll catch up with you in a minute," I said. He left and I walked over to Ms. Bristol, who was now sitting at her desk.

She said in a low voice, "Have you given my visit much thought?"

I wasn't quite sure how to respond, so I simply nodded and gave a short, "I have."

"And you haven't mentioned it to anyone, correct? Not even Mason?" she asked.

"No ma'am. Of course not," I said respectfully.

"Big game today, huh?" she asked scanning my attire. "Is it going to be a tough one?"

We were playing our rival school, East High Bulldogs. It'd been three years since our school had beat them. They had a team stacked with giants. We had a team of average Joes. The only hope we had this year was a few good shooters. The David to their Goliaths. I'd like to think of myself as one of those good shooters, but we'd see in tonight's game.

"Yeah, we'll need to play at our best to win this one," I said truthfully.

She finished by telling me she might stop by to watch for a bit and wished me good luck.

As I stepped out of Ms. Bristol's classroom, I noticed Mason sitting on the ground with his back against the wall, fiddling with his cellphone. He heard me approaching and shot up with a quizzical look on his face, "What was that about?"

I figured Mason would ask exactly that, so I had an answer ready for him, "She wanted to make sure her curriculum wasn't 'boring' me. She said I looked distracted for most of her lecture." I hated lying in general, but it was even worse lying to my best friend. Especially when the lying came so easily. "I just told her I was thinking about the game." At least there was some truth to what I was saying.

Seeming satisfied with my explanation, Mason asked, "Are you nervous? The team hasn't beat these guys in, what, over three years?"

I told Mason I was a little nervous, because I honestly was. I had a very competitive edge to me. I wanted to win and three years in a row of losing was a hard pill to swallow. I don't think I could take another year, so for the rest of school I lingered in my thoughts with a small shroud like feeling of anxiety looming over me.

"You going to stay and watch?" I asked Mason. He didn't always. Sometimes he used that time to go home, lock himself in his room, and fidget with his gadgets.

"I think so, it's a big game," he said.

Mason enjoyed sports, he simply enjoyed technology more. Not to mention that he wasn't exactly built like an athlete.

As we were chatting Woody came walking around the corner with his arm around Tenzie. She didn't pay any attention to us, but Woody did.

"Oh, would you look at that. Short stack who thinks he's the next Steph Curry and his nerdy sidekick," he jabbed.

It was such a dumb comment, I debated even responding but I let my ego get the best of me and said, "I see you found Fiona, where's your two donkeys, Shrek?"

His face deepened to a red tone as blood rushed to his cheeks. Pure rage and embarrassment unfolding. He'd removed his arm from around Tenzie and stepped in front of me. I couldn't tell if he was going to hit me or spit in my face. Considering I didn't feel pain, I was hoping for him to hit me.

He towered over me. Ready to strike. I braced for it. Ready to retaliate. He pulled his fist back.

"Is there a problem here?" a sharp voice cut through the tension in the hall.

All four of us, Woody, Tenzie, Mason, and I turned in unison to see Ms. Bristol walking briskly toward us.

I don't know what she would've done, but Woody didn't give us the chance to find out.

"Have fun losing again, Freddy Krueger," he said in reference to all my scars, then he gave me a quick shove and walked in the opposite direction of Ms. Bristol.

By the time she got to us Woody and Tenzie had disappeared around the corner.

Ms. Bristol stopped in front of us and with a hand on her hip said, "Don't you gentleman have somewhere to be?"

We nodded and left without any further discussion.

After school I went straight to the locker room to get changed and start mentally preparing for the game. I was the first and only one in there. As I waited for my teammates to show up I walked over to the sink and splashed some water in my face, trying to calm myself down as pregame nerves began creeping in.

When the water was wiped away from my face, I stared back at my reflection in the mirror that showed me from the waist up. In my basketball jersey with no sleeves I was able to see how horrific my arms looked. They were muscular but covered with years and years of collected scars. Not good-looking scars either. They were a variety of thick and thin scars. Raised and not raised. Clumped together in random spots all over my arms.

One by one my teammates started filing in to get changed and ready for the game. Our coach was the last to arrive. Derrick Memphis, to us Coach Memphis, was new this year to being our coach. He was brought in to completely revamp the basketball program and get us back on track. We'd played some smaller schools and got some wins under our belt, but today's game would be the real challenge. While other schools were looking for the tallest, biggest kids to build a team, Coach Memphis was looking for talent; players that could dribble well and shoot better.

After a quick motivational speech Coach Memphis snagged a blue marker and wrote the starting line up on the whiteboard. Listing me as the starting point guard. I'd been battling for that position against Blake Adams, a senior, so it was a relief to see my hard work had paid off.

Huddled up, we did a quick chant then ran out on the court to begin warmups. Because East High was no more than a twenty-minute drive from us, half our gym was filled with their fans. Taunting us as we ran up for layups and singing their school song in an effort to drown out our fans. Even though I was nervous I loved the anticipation and excitement before a game. It was a fun, energetic atmosphere.

The game began and the Bulldogs wasted no time getting points on the board. We'd score a basket then they'd score two. Slowly the game was getting away from us.

While the Bulldogs' power forward was taking a foul shot, I glanced around the stadium and noticed a few things. The first thing I noticed was Ms. Bristol, standing out like a rose amongst weeds. She'd made it to the game. The second thing I noticed was Woody, Scott, and Todd. They were just beyond the bleachers harassing a pretty girl wearing a Bulldogs' T-shirt and Tenzie was nowhere in sight. I wondered what she would think about her boyfriend hitting on another girl. The last thing I noticed was Blake Adams stretching out his arms and looking over at Coach Memphis with a look that asked, "Time for me to come off the bench yet?"

I knew I had to do something, or I'd be heading over to the bench for the rest of the game. The Bulldogs' player made both free throws and one of our players tossed the ball into me. I dribbled up the court at a fast pace, not wasting anytime. At half court a Bulldogs' player tried to defend me. I crossed over the ball and blew right past him. Another player ran up to stop me. I faked a pass that sent him in the other direction and pulled up to shoot five feet off the three-point line. A high arch sent the ball soaring through the net for three points.

I directed the team to full court press. The Bulldogs went to throw the ball in, and I intercepted it to lay it up for two points.

Basket by basket, point by point, we inched closer to taking the lead.

By the time the third quarter ended we'd taken our first lead of the game. It was 78 to 75. Huddled on the bench, Coach Memphis informed me that Blake would be finishing out the game. Explaining that as a senior it was his last opportunity to play our rival school. I'd been benched, and not for the benefit of the team. We ended up losing the game. Blake only put up two points and we lost by twelve, keeping the Bulldogs win streak against us alive.

Chapter 9

After another one of my mother's delicious dinners I was hand washing the dishes when my father's cellphone, sitting on the kitchen counter, began to ring. It was an unknown number.

My father who was bringing in the dirty dishes from the table noticed the vibrating phone and picked it up.

I wasn't able to hear whoever was on the other end of the line, but my father stayed in the kitchen to talk so I was at least able to hear his side of the conversation.

"Hello? Yes, this is he. Uh-huh…" he said. There was a minute or so of silence on his end, then, "I see. Definitely something to talk about. We'll be in touch. Thank you. And you do the same."

Clicking off the call he turned to me, "Where's your mother? We all need to sit down and talk."

I never liked the sound of that, but responded, "I'll go grab her."

Dirty dishes abandoned and sitting in the living room with my father positioned opposite of my mother and I, my father told us that the call was from Ms. Bristol. He said she'd decided they'd like to extend an official offer for me to join the S.I.C. program. Which meant it was ultimately up to us to decide if we wanted to accept such an offer or not.

My parents, being the great parents that they were, told me it was my life so ultimately it was my decision. I already knew my answer. I'd stewed over it since the night of Ms. Bristol's visit.

"So, what do you think champ? It's a great opportunity, but we'll sure miss the hell out of you," my father said not pushing me toward one way or the other.

I watched my mother fret nervously, occasionally biting at her fingernails. I knew what she wanted, but was it the same thing I wanted?

I inhaled and exhaled a deep breath and said, "I'll take my chances..." I looked at my mother, the worry on her face, "... outside of the program." My mother's face lit up. As did my father's.

"Are you sure?" my mother asked. "You're not just saying that for my sake?"

"Partially," I said, with a witty smile. "But I also like my life as is and I don't want things to change. I can always go to one of the three colleges close by and make a name for myself. I don't need some secret government program to be someone."

"Then it's decided," my father said clapping his hands together. "I'll call Ms. Bristol and let her know." He stood up and left the room to do so.

The phone call with Ms. Bristol didn't last very long because my father was right back in the room with us no more than a minute later, grinning from ear to ear. It appeared both of my parents were ecstatic with my decision. Honestly, I felt good about it too.

Instead of running off to my room to get lost in my book, I decided to hang out with my parents for a while and enjoy a movie in their company. They'd been good to me my entire life. Family was everything to me and I simply couldn't give that up.

* * *

The weekend arrived and Mason and I made plans to scrounge up some dollars and go see what new comics we could find. After our last ordeal hunting, we were hoping for a more laid-back weekend.

Originally our only plans for the day were going to Page Turners for comic books and that was it but being that it was midafternoon, and our stomachs were grumbling, we made a pitstop at a sandwich shop.

It was a popular place called Ned's Breads. Popular because while most sandwich shops were stingy on the meat, Ned's was extremely generous; and fairly priced. Which is how a couple broke kids like us, who didn't receive allowances from their parents, could afford it and still have some left over change for comic books.

I scarfed down a cheddar and barbecue brisket and Mason nearly finished a meatball sub. With our hunger satisfied and each with a Coke in hand, we walked out the door to head over to Page Turners.

It was a nice enough day. The sun was out, and the streets were filled with people coming and going from various stores and restaurants. To get to Page Turners from the sandwich shop we had to cut through an alley. An alley that in any other town would seem really sketchy. Our town, however, had a low crime rate and was overall pretty safe. That's why Mason and I had no problem cutting through the alley. An alley that displayed garbage spilled from dumpsters and hid mice in shadows.

The mice weren't the only thing hidden in the shadows of the alley. Next to an old dented dumpster, sprayed with graffiti, there was a large lump.

I walked in front and Mason edged behind me as we approached the lump. Slowly it started to rise and the lump on the ground transformed into a full-grown man.

"Charles?" I said to the now stretching man, arms spread wide above his head.

"Hi Fellas," Charles drawled.

Charles Bodart was a man on hard times. Surprisingly, homeless in an alley, tucked away by a smelly dumpster, wasn't the hardest of times Charles h
ad fallen on.

Charles' wife was taken from him years ago. Some form of cancer and when they found out she was ill it was only months before she was gone. With his wife ripped from his life abruptly and a hole in his heart, Charles attempted to take his own life. He was found hanging from a sheet in his bedroom when his wife's brother came to check on him shortly after. He survived but the lack of oxygen caused some brain damage. The brain damage cost Charles his job. Losing his job cost him his home. A continuous downward spiral.

The whole town knew Charles and his story and tried to help out where they could, but the person that was left after all the damage was bitter and refused help from most. The only kindness he'd allow Mason and I to offer was the occasional food we'd bring by.

Mason always felt a little uneasy around Charles like he was a rubber band pulled tight, ready to snap at any moment. I imagined most people felt that way. I enjoyed Charles though and was never too worried about it.

I took off my backpack and fished in it for the two bags of chips we'd gotten with our meal but decided not to eat so we could give them to Charles.

I tossed him the two bags and he looked them over before saying, "Salt an' Vinny an' plains potato chip. My favorites. Thanks fellas. You always so kind to bring me food. I thanks you both."

We both offered a sincere 'You're welcome' and I handed him the Coke I'd refilled to the brim.

"Enjoy," I said as we left and continued on toward Page Turners.

Page Turners was surprisingly busy when we got there. All types of customers searching through various genres to find the right novel. The smell of coffee mixed with freshly printed pages to create an aroma only found in bookstores.

We passed by the romance section that was an empty aisle at the moment, through the horror section where an elderly gentleman was skimming through a Stephen King novel, to our DC and Marvel universe in the back.

To my surprise Lance Turner had replaced the Thor cutout with a Wonder Woman one. She was positioned sideways with a golden lasso draped between her hands as if she were about to throw it.

I couldn't help but think that the move to put up a woman, and one from the DC realm, was a ploy to make more sales. I couldn't fault Mr. Turner for it though and whatever his motives were, at least it was a step in the right direction.

Wanting a break from my normal reading material I decided to sift through the Flash and Aquaman comics in the 'clearance' section. Mason also looked in the clearance section, but he was hunting for a specific comic book that was part of the Dark Knight series.

After both of us found the comics we wanted to purchase we left Page Turners and headed back toward the sandwich shop where we'd left our bikes locked up.

We cut back through the alley and the first thing I noticed was the smashed bag of chips and the fountain drink spilled amongst the other trash on the ground, which was strange because there still seemed to be a lot of chips left in the bag and quite a bit of soda spilled. Charles was always appreciative of the food we brought him and usually polished it off with no problem, but as we got closer to the dumpsters, I realized that Charles wasn't alone.

We stepped around the sticky mess of soda and chips, Mason edging behind me again, and came around the dumpsters to see Woody, Todd, and Scott standing over a bleeding Charles.

"What's going on?" I asked genuinely curious and worried about Charles.

Woody didn't waste any time in responding, "Nothing that concerns you. Mind your own business and get out of here."

With what little light broke through the alley's darkness, I could see dark spots splattered across Woody's shirt. I looked to Todd and Scott who also had these dark blotches.

I ran over to Charles who laid limp. There was so much blood I couldn't tell where it was coming from.

Mason had his phone out and was dialing 911 when either Todd or Scott rushed him, shouting, "Oh no you don't!"

They tumbled to the ground and all I could see was arms flailing about as Mason struggled to get Todd or Scott off him. The other Todd or Scott ran over to assist in holding down Mason.

While all that was happening, I turned toward Woody. I had rage in my heart for Charles and what they'd done to him. So much rage it shined through my eyes as they bore down on Woody, "Why?" A one-word question that held so much.

Woody chuckled and shrugged, "He wouldn't give us the bag of chips."

I looked back to Charles who was taking long, heavy breathes. I couldn't quite wrap my head around it. They'd beat a man senseless over a bag of chips. A man with brain damage who kept to himself and did nothing to them.

I couldn't feel pain, but I could feel anger. A fiery red deep within took control of my actions. I became a robot controlled by emotion. All logic and reason gone. I had one simple motive. Hurt those that hurt Charles.

I scooped up the other bag of chips that laid smashed close to Charles, grinding chips between my fingers. Woody watched me curiously. Time slowed. Quickly, I grabbed a handful of the broken chips, small pieces

that were a few crunches away from being dust and
threw the chips in Woody's face.

His eyes must have been opened, because he
groaned in pain and rubbed at them. I took this
opportunity to kick off one of the dumpsters, that
screeched an awful noise as it scratched against the
pavement, and right hooked Woody. I connected with
his temple.

Woody hit the ground and didn't move. Todd and
Scott let go of Mason and slowly walked over to the
still body of their friend. Mason looked for his phone.
Charles groaned. I looked down at my fist, still
clenched tight.

Chapter 10

I don't know how long I sat there staring at my fist, frozen in shock. I didn't unclench it until Mason touched me on the shoulder.

"Are you okay?" he asked.

I wasn't sure what I was. My brain strained to recall the last 30 seconds. Then I remembered Charles and turned to assist him, since it appeared Todd and Scott were assisting Woody.

He was in bad shape. His left eye drooping awkwardly and turning a dark purple blended with a maroon color. His tattered clothes were covered in fresh blood that dripped from his nose. His frail, nutrient lacking arms failed to hold him up as he dropped on his side.

"Just relax, we'll get you help," I said to him.

Mason said he'd called 911 and they were on the way.

"He's dead," came a whisper from either Todd or Scott.

I wanted to believe that they were talking about Charles, so I could correct them and tell them 'no, he wasn't dead. Just hurt really bad.' But, in my gut I knew they weren't talking about Charles.

I numbly walked over to where Woody lay. Thinking that maybe they were mistaken, and he was simply unconscious. That false hope left me as soon as I saw his body. Skin that was once a dark peachy tone, now had a gray hue to it. He was still. No chest heaving up and down. Just still. I stuck my finger under his nostrils just to be sure. No breath touched my finger. I felt for a pulse. Nothing. He was dead.

I suddenly felt sick. The cheddar brisket churning inside me. I leaned over the dumpster and threw up all the contents in my stomach. Then I leaned up against the wall and gradually slumped to the ground. Oblivious to what the others were doing around me. I'm not sure how long I sat there, but I didn't look up until the alleyway was teeming with paramedics and policemen.

A larger officer approached me while a few other officers rounded up the others. The paramedics had already hauled away Charles and Woody. Charles on a stretcher and Woody in a body bag.

"Son," the large officer said to me, "I'm going to need you to come with me."

I didn't respond or protest. I just stood up and followed the large officer out of the alley. He didn't attempt to cuff me, but he did stay really close; should I get the nerve to try anything.

Outside of the alley a small cluster of people began to form, trying to see what was going on. The large officer directed me to the back of his cruiser and shut the door.

I watched the crowd of people murmur amongst themselves and snap photos with their phones. Yet, my mind was put on hold. I didn't register my surroundings. I was only existing. I wasn't producing any thoughts. No thinking of the future or the past. I was just there. Stuck in that moment. I don't even recall how I ended up in a holding cell at the local police station, but it was there that my mind slowly started working again. It was there that the reality of what I had done hit me.

I'd killed someone. One moment Woody was alive and moving, joking with his pals at the expense of Charles. The next, he was dead. Lifeless. One punch to end two lives. Mine and his. I was going away for the rest of my life and I knew it.

I wondered if my parents knew I was here. I'm sure by now the whole town knew. The way gossip spread in these parts.

The cell they held me in was all cement with a steel table and a glass window, just like in the movies. There were cuffs connected to the center of the table, but again, the officer didn't bother putting them on. Maybe because I was just a kid or maybe because he knew I wasn't going anywhere. He left me in the cell alone for quite some time. It felt like hours.

The first person to enter the cell was the last person I expected.

Ms. Bristol strolled in all business like and as gorgeous as ever. I struggled to make sense of why she was here. She held a cup of what looked and smelled like coffee. She sat down across from me and slid the steaming drink toward me.

"I'm sure you could use a pick me up," she said with a face that showed no emotion at all. "Probably something even stronger than this, but this is the best I can do."

I took a moment to enjoy a swig of the coffee. I didn't know if I'd ever have such a luxury again. Then I said, "I don't understand. Why are you here?" I didn't mean it rude. I was genuinely curious. What was a schoolteacher doing in the jail cell I was being held in for murdering another student? This was a little bigger than an incident at school. This was a job for policemen and lawyers. Not schoolteachers and government recruiters, or whatever her real title was.

"We'll get into that momentarily," she began. "I've helped your parents locate a lawyer for you."

"My parents!" I belted out. "Are they here? Do they know what happened???"

"Lucas," she said in a soft tone that belonged to a psychiatrist, not a schoolteacher. "Calm down for a minute and let me explain how this is going to work."

I took a deep breath and nodded. Ready to listen.

She went on, "Your parents are outside and they're
aware of the situation. The lawyer we've obtained for
you is going to come in and talk to you about your
options. Your parents have already signed off on it.
You don't need to give him an answer right away.
After he's laid out your options your parents are going
to come in. You'll have five minutes with them to
discuss. Then the lawyer will return and expect you to
have an answer. Do you understand?"

I didn't fully understand. I wasn't in the right state of
mind for any of this, but I nodded my head yes so that
we could get through this and I could see my parents.
I needed to see them. I needed to explain myself. I
needed them on my side.

"Ok then," Ms. Bristol said. "I'll go grab the lawyer."

Ms. Bristol stood up and left the room. When she
returned, an older gentleman that was balding on top
and had a salt and pepper beard followed after her.
He introduced himself as Arnold Hammond (Arnie for
short), attorney at law. He was a heavier set man with
the thickest lenses I'd ever seen, but he played the
part well; he had an expensive looking black suit and
a vocabulary that left me scratching my head.

After the small introductions and a brief lesson on
how the law worked, he got into the specifics, "There
was enough witnesses to get a good idea of what
happened today. The good news is, we know they're
not going to charge you with first degree murder
because none of this was premeditated. The bad
news is, you weren't the one being attacked when you

decided to punch Mark Woods so we can't plead for self-defense. Which means the charge will fall somewhere in between. Because that punch resulted in death, you're going to be charged with either manslaughter or second-degree murder. Both would require prison time. Manslaughter being the lesser of the two would have you looking at four years in this state. That's assuming everything goes flawlessly in court. Here, second degree murder is a minimum of fifteen years in prison."

My life was over. No matter what, I was going to prison. I had an idea of this in the back of my mind, but hearing the lawyer say it with such certainty just solidified my knowledge that I'd be going away.

Arnie let his words sit in the silence of my sorrow for a moment, then said, "However, with that being said."

I looked up at him, a small twinkle of hope in my eyes. Possibly another option? A way out of this?

"With that being said, there is a way out of being charged at all," Arnie spoke to me but glanced over at Ms. Bristol.

I didn't understand. They could see the confusion sprinkled with hope on my face as Arnie said, "Vera, would you like to do the honors of telling Lucas the other option?" It sounded funny hearing Ms. Bristol called by her first name.

"I'd love to," she said to Arnie, then turned to me, "There's a way you can avoid prison time altogether."

I didn't say anything, but my hope for a way out was growing.

"The solution would be that you enter the Skilled Individuals' Community. The S.I.C. program," she said it like it was so simple.

Confused, I asked, "How is that a possibility? I don't understand."

Ms. Bristol smiled, "It's a possibility because the S.I.C. program is funded and put on by the United States government and we want you as a candidate. I must warn you though, there are stipulations to this deal because of the circumstances, if you should choose to enter the program you will be completely cut off from your parents and your old life; which is over anyway. You will be expected to remain and associate within the community. After you complete the program, we can look at reuniting you with your parents. The duration of the program will depend on how fast you progress. If you're a fast learner, it won't take you long to finish the program and see your parents again."

I considered what she was telling me, "So you're saying I could choose to join this program for 'skilled individuals' over prison time, but I wouldn't be able to see or communicate with my parents?"

She nodded yes, but didn't say anything else.

Arnie chimed in, "It's a lucky break kid, but ultimately it has to be your decision. You've got to tell us what you'd like to do."

"As I told you earlier, we're going to leave now and let your parents come in for five minutes so you can discuss," Ms. Bristol began standing up as she said this, and Arnie followed.

Moments later my parents walked in with sorrowful faces and tear stained cheeks. Both had been crying. My father's tears stung the most. I'd never seen my father cry.

At first, nothing was said. They just alternated giving me hugs. Then my father with a cracking voice said, "You don't need to tell us what happened. We know the boy we raised, and we know you were defending Charles. For that we're forever proud of you. We're sorry that your stuck with this ultimatum of joining this program or going to prison and since it's your life, it's your choice but we will offer our opinion. Which is, take the deal for the program. It puts you in a better position for the future. Prison only digs you a hole in life that you'll forever have to climb out of."

My mother gave a similar speech to my father's, we hugged some more. My mother planted a few kisses and then Ms. Bristol came back to lead them out.

It seemed to be an obvious decision for everyone else, but I still considered seeing what I was charged with. If it was manslaughter, I could be out in four years and communicate with my parents the whole time. Even if it was through a glass window. If I chose the program, then they were gone from my life for who knows how long.

Ms. Bristol and Arnie sat across from me, waiting for an answer. I could see a stack of papers Arnie held in front of him that were titled: **S.I.C. Program Agreement.**

I told them my decision and asked for a pen to begin signing my life away.

The S.I.C. Program

Book Two

<u>Chapter 1</u>

I laid on the bed in my jail cell, grateful that I was unable to feel aches and pain. Because judging by the stiffness of the bed, I'm sure anyone else would be throbbing right about now. The small cell definitely wasn't designed for the inmate's benefit.

I was physically exhausted but couldn't find sleep due to my wandering mind. In the near future I would have a whole new life. A life away from my parents, my best friend, and everything I've known up until this point.

I suddenly felt the urge to move. I hopped out of bed and began pacing the perimeter of the small cell. That's when I heard footsteps that weren't mine. Someone was coming.

The footsteps were slow and heavy. Whoever it was, they were in no rush. A minute or so later, the person the footsteps belonged to arrived at my cell. He was a short man that was built like a running back; broad as he was tall.

Surprisingly, he wasn't dressed in any sort of uniform. He wore Converse tennis shoes, Levi's, and a plain white shirt. He must have been some form of a cop though, because he had keys to my cell. He unlocked it and told me to follow him. After tossing the keys to a local officer that was sitting at the front desk and blowing on his coffee, he escorted me out the side door of the police station.

Outside, a white van with midnight black tint was waiting for us. He opened the back door, told me to take a seat and buckle up. I'd still yet to be cuffed. Which I didn't mind. I did as I was told, and the van pulled out into the night with me as a passenger. I was now property of the United States government.

We drove for hours. The stout man barely said a word to me the whole drive and I didn't mind in the slightest. All I wanted now was sleep and I finally found it.

As sunlight broke through the tinted windows, I began to wake. I gave my eyes a moment to adjust then I took in my surroundings. We were in the middle of a city. Far larger than my hometown. There were buildings so tall that the tops of them were hidden in clouds. People of all different sizes and shapes moved about on the street. Cars honked, music played, and people shouted. It was a little overwhelming taking in all the noise and the hustle and bustle of the people around me.

As we drove the buildings began to get smaller and apartments and townhomes took their places. We turned into a neighborhood of townhomes packed tightly together. They were colored vibrantly with blues, reds, yellows. You name it. It was a very colorful row of homes. I'd never seen houses colored so bright.

We pulled up to a blue townhouse and the man driving hit a button on his visor to open up the two-car garage.

We pulled into what appeared to be like any other garage. Cement flooring and a door to the house. Thinking we'd reached our final destination I unbuckled and opened the door.

"Hey!" the man shouted back at me.

I looked at him puzzled.

"Get back in the car. We're not there yet," he said.

I was confused but sat back down.

"Put the seatbelt back on," he said with a serious look on his face.

I did as I was told and waited for whatever was going to happen next. The man pulled out his cellphone and began pushing something on it. Next, I felt a small jolt as the van moved. Except it wasn't the van. The garage door was now closed behind us. There was nowhere for the van to go.

I glanced out the window and saw the floor lowering. We were going down. Like we were on some sort of platform being lowered into the ground.

When the floor stopped moving a tunnel sat in front of us. With plenty of space for the van to fit. The ceiling of the tunnel held canned lights the whole length of the drive. It took us about thirty minutes to get to the end of it.

At the end of the tunnel the man told me to climb out. I did as I was told. Once I was out of the van, I watched the man turn the van around and leave. I was stunned, confused. I thought about running after the van, then decided against it. There must have been a reason he'd left me here. That's when I noticed it.

In the corner of the wall there was a blinking light. A light that belonged to a camera. I was being watched.

I scanned the area some more and noticed some discoloration on the wall that ended the tunnel. I swiped my finger over the discoloration, and it came back with paint on it. As if someone had just repaired the wall.

With nowhere else to go I figured this must be it, but why was I left here to figure this out? Was it some sort of test? I didn't have any answers, but with the camera on me I figured it was best to act; just in case my inclines were right.

I pulled back my leg and kicked at the freshly painted wall. Nothing happened. So, I kicked harder. This time my leg broke through and I nearly fell to my death but ended up catching myself on a ladder. The ladder descended quite a way down a small shaft. Rung by rung I lowered myself into the unknown. Into complete darkness.

After what felt like twenty minutes of climbing down
the ladder, my shoes stepped onto solid ground.
There was no light. It was as if I'd descended to the
dark depths of hell. It was hot, sweat collected at my
armpits and dripped from my brow, and it was quiet.
An eerie sort of quiet.

With no cellphone on me for light I felt around
aimlessly in the dark until my hand landed on a
doorknob. I turned the knob and subtle light began
spilling out of the cracked door. I stepped into the
room and waited a moment for my eyes to adjust.

It was a simple cement room with low lighting from a
bulb that dangled from the ceiling. Opposite of where I
entered was an elevator. The elevator had an up and
a down button. I failed to see the purpose in the
strange architectural layout thus far but noticed
another blinking camera in the corner and concluded
it must be some sort of admissions test, so I
proceeded.

In front of the elevator was a small round table with a
note on it. The note read:

*Here you leave your old life behind and start new. If
you haven't figured it out already, this is a test. So,
pick a button; up or down. What you choose tells us a
lot about you. But choose wisely, because the
direction you choose determines your future.*

I stood a moment contemplating which button to
press. Watching the blinking light in my peripheral.
Thinking that this test could be timed and that that

factored into my test results, I quickly pressed the down button.

The elevator doors opened up and I stepped inside. There were no buttons on the inside, but there was another camera. I felt the elevator start to ascend, which confused me because I'd most definitely pressed the down button.

As the elevator went up, I began to realize the purpose of the tunnels, the ladder, the darkness, and the elevator. The strange architectural design was simply a way to keep the Skilled Individuals' Community hidden from outsiders. My guess was this was a test to see if you could get to the community. I wouldn't be surprised if they had these entrances all over the city. Probably testing others right now.

I wasn't ready for the next part of the test. The elevator stopped and the doors opened to another cement room that was similar to the one I'd just come from. Another dim light bulb hung from the ceiling and beneath it was a man.

At least I assumed it was a man, judging by the broad shoulders and the way he was sitting. He was sitting in a chair with his arms tied behind his back and his legs wide, where a woman's legs would more likely be held closer together or overlapping. His head was covered with a bag and slack against his chest. He looked dead or injured badly.

I approached the man with caution. When I was close enough, I noticed a note that looked like it had fallen from his lap and now sat on the floor. Waiting for me to read it. I picked the note up and read:

This is the passage. You must grab an item from the bag in the corner and use it to end this man's life. Don't worry about your soul. This man deserves what's coming to him. He's guilty of unspeakable crimes. Complete this task and join the others in the community. Do not complete the task and you will reside in a federal prison for the remainder of your life for treason.

I could hardly believe what I had just read. I scanned the small room. There was a knapsack bag in the corner and no other way out except the elevator I came in on. The only other thing I noticed in the room was another blinking camera in the corner.

Were they serious? They expected me to kill this man? I was here because I killed a man. Now I was being asked to do it again? What was the S.I.C. Program really?

I walked to the corner and picked up the bag. Checking it's contents I found a small handgun, a syringe needle filled with a thick brown liquid, a hammer, and a piece of rope.

This was more like the game of Clue than real life; pick your murder weapon. I couldn't do it.

"I'm not a murderer," I pleaded to the camera, but nothing happened. The man sat slack and the room remained silent. For almost an hour I sat there contemplating what to do.

Then I began to wonder about the man in the chair. Who was he? What had he done? How could his crimes be worse than murder? My crime.

I was beginning to realize that I didn't have a life anymore. I didn't have a choice anymore. The government owned me. I was now their property. Their product. And what sort of product were they making me into?

I looked over the four items again. A gun, some sort of poison, a hammer, and a rope.

I wasn't a barbarian, so I put the hammer and rope back into the bag. I looked back and forth between the gun and the poison. Wondering what type of poison was it? A slow killing one? The thought of having to watch the man die slowly bothered me, so I put the syringe needle back in the bag as well.

I checked the gun to see if there had been any bullets loaded. There was one.

I tapped the gun against the cement floor. Clank, clank, clank. Slowly building up the courage to go through with it. Then rapidly I stood, placed the gun against the man's head, that was still hidden from view beneath the bag, and fired.

The sound was deafening in the small room. Slowly a red circle formed against the cream color of the bag.

Chapter 2

The elevator opened behind me and Ms. Bristol entered clapping her hands. "Well done, Lucas. Well done."

She removed the bag from the man's head and blank eyes stared back at me. There was a dark crimson hole where I'd shot the man in the forehead above his right eye.

I felt the nausea again, but this time I stomached it and remained standing with a sense of confidence.

"What were his crimes?" I asked.

Ms. Bristol smiled, "I guess you've earned that. He was a Russian Mafia member who ran a sex trafficking business, a rapist, a mass murderer, and one of America's most wanted. You did your country a favor, so thank you."

Ms. Bristol gestured for me to follow her back into the elevator. Seeing as it was the only way out. This time it went down.

Inside the elevator Ms. Bristol turned to me with a seriousness about her, "Lucas, I need you to understand something."

For some reason, I felt like I already knew what she was going to say.

She waited until she knew I was listening, "I know I may have given you some false hope when we had our initial discussions with your parents, but I need you to know now… your old life… your parents… your friends. That's a thing of the past. A memory. Those people, unfortunately, are not a part of your future. No matter what happens in the S.I.C. program, you can never go back. The government will prevent that. There's always a cover story, buried beneath a bigger conspiracy. There's no way out except to succeed here. I'm rooting for you."

Before I could respond the elevator, doors opened. Opened to a new world. A new life.

Just as Ms. Bristol had described to my parents the community grounds looked like an old-school college campus. The only thing she forgot to mention was that it was all underground. A whole town underground.

Streets alive with people. Buildings. Yes, buildings beneath buildings. It was incredible. Mom-and-Pop shops just like back home. Restaurants. Everything one would see in a regular town.

It was as sunny as if there were a real sun. The ceiling imitated the sky, but if you stared long enough it was easy to tell it wasn't actually the sun. Some sort of digital imitation. Still, it was amazing.

I followed Ms. Bristol across a nicely groomed lawn, also fake, to a building designed from red brick. More stout than tall. It was central in the town, which made me believe it held some importance. That and the fact that there were people coming from all different directions to get to the building.

Inside was a large auditorium. The auditorium was built downward like a large crater lined with seats. The outside of the building was deceptive to the true size of the auditorium.

There was a stage that held a podium at the bottom of all the seating. The seating was divided into four sections. Each section had a banner hanging above it.

The banner furthest from us was royal purple with a white skull and crossbones. Behind the skull and crossbones were a few pink flowers. I recognized the flowers from a cheesy Netflix film where the killer used them to poison her victims. I believe they called them Oleanders, but I wasn't sure. All I knew was that they were poisonous. On the bottom of the banner there were three white letters: D.M.P.

The section next to that had a solid black banner with a tan fist clenching a short blade tactical knife. At the bottom of this banner were the white letters: D.P.A.

The next banner was a matte gray color with red cross hairs in the middle. Towards the bottom of the cross hairs there was lettering in black and read: L.D.K.

The last section housed a gold banner. It was the smallest of the four sections with no one currently sitting there. On this banner was a gray brain and black letters that read: G.M.E.

Behind the podium was more seating. Where people of all ages continued to file in. Above the podium hung a Jumbotron; a large display that had video feedback of those on the stage. Ms. Bristol led me down to one of the seats towards the back of the stage and told me to sit tight and that the orientation would begin shortly. I watched her find seating at the front of the stage amongst, what I assumed to be, other staff members.

An elderly gentleman, whose skin hung loosely on his frail body, stood and slowly approached the podium. It was easy to see he was a taller man during his younger years because of the long arms and lanky legs, but now he hunched over so far that inches were taken off his overall height.

He used the podium to straighten himself and put on a pair of glasses to read some notes he'd removed from the inner pocket of his suit coat.

As they zoomed in on his face and showcased it across the Jumbotron, I got the feeling that I'd seen this gentleman before.

When the man introduced himself as Ronald Huffington, I realized I had seen this man before. On the television giving a speech. He was the Secretary of Defense.

The auditorium was intensely quiet with respect for the speaker and the anticipation of what we'd be learning about the future of our lives.

Ronald's voice was deep with a touch of hoarseness, but it carried well across the auditorium and his articulation was impressive. One of a man who'd given many public speeches over the years.

"New recruits," is how he addressed us as he started his speech.

While he was going over a brief history of the institution and how the S.I.C. program came about the man next to me leaned over. He looked to be in his early twenties and an avid gym goer. He looked like a guy who belonged in the military. Maybe he was.

"How'd you kill your guy, little man? And how'd you get all those scars?" he asked me in a hushed tone.

So apparently everyone did go through a similar passage to be a part of the S.I.C program. The man seemed arrogant. Sure of himself. I didn't like that.

"Quick and painless," was all I said, ignoring the question about my scars.

He smiled, revealing a perfect set off chompers, "Ah, used the gun then huh? Typical, but you're just a boy so I can't blame you. Although when I was your age I was prepping to be shipped overseas for some hand-to-hand combat."

I wondered how old he thought I was.

"What did you use?" I asked.

His smile remained as he said, "Hammer of course. I wanted to feel the vibrating of the handle as I took down my target. Reminds me that I'm the one doing the dirty deed. Harder to disassociate, which forces you to live with the guilt; which ultimately makes you stronger."

This dude sounded like an animal. How could you beat someone with a hammer then sit and have casual conversation about it?

I turned my attention back to the speaker. He was turning to look at us on the stage, "Newcomers, it is time to learn which division you will be a part of during your duration with the community. But first, congratulations to all of you for making it here. You had very little guidance yet made it to the community."

He turned back to those under the banners, "Now before we find out which division our newcomers are a part of it is important to know the different divisions."

Ronald extended an arm toward the section with the purple banner, "The first section over here is the Division of Many Poisons or as their sign suggests: D.M.P. I will go more in depth on these divisions in a moment. Next to D.M.P we have the Division of Physical Ability or as their sign reads: D.P.A. If you haven't noticed, our government loves their

abbreviations. Following D.P.A. we have the Long-Distance Killers division or L.D.K."
Ronald cleared his throat, "Lastly, we have our Gray Matter Elitists aka G.M.E."

Ronald let his words sink in a moment before going on, "If you haven't figured it out by now, I'll lay it out in laymen's terms for you. This. Is. Assassin school. Each one of you has been handpicked by one of our recruiters because of some potential they saw in you, a special skill, or maybe some misfortune that's allowed us to give you a second chance. Whatever the reason, you're here now and we're going to train you to be elite soldiers so that when you're done with the program you can walk right into a government job protecting your country. Your service starts now."

"Assassin school?" I repeated softly to myself. Suddenly it all made sense. They'd made us kill as a way of getting into the program. Every person here was a killer. Now they'd gotten that out of the way they might as well train us and use us for our country's benefit. I could hardly believe it. Our government was creating killers, subtly underground. A secret group of killers off the public record. Essentially unknown to the public. The possibilities for this group were limitless.

The Secretary of Defense went on, "Your killing method is what determines your division. Each recruit was given the option to kill with either a hammer, a rope, a gun, or a syringe of poison."

The brute next to me whispered, "Well looks like you and I are going to be in different sections. I'd tell you my name's Devin, but I guess it hardly matters now so I won't even bother asking yours. Best of luck to you soldier."

I just nodded; grateful we wouldn't be in the same group.

"Those that killed their subject with the syringe will be going to the Division of Many Poisons," Ronald said. "This is a pretty obvious one. Members in this group prefer not to see the effects of their killing, yet don't particularly care what suffering their victim undergoes. New recruits that belong in the D.MP section are now being displayed on the Jumbotron and you may now join your division."

A third of the newcomers on stage shuffled over to the D.M.P section after seeing their name. Devin and I remained seated.

"The recruits that killed their subject with the hammer are better suited for our D.P.A group. These types of killers don't mind blood on their hands and almost prefer it to other killing methods. It's proof to them of what they've done. These individuals are well equipped for close combat. See the names above and join your section."

This time Devin didn't say anything to me. He just hopped up excitedly and joined his division.

"The ones who used the rope to kill are a little more complicated and harder to predict. These individuals belong to the Long-Distance Killers and I know what you're thinking, killing someone with a rope is the opposite of a long-distance kill. This is true, but similar to a long-distance kill, most of those that used the rope did it by strangling the victim from behind or making a noose and kicking the chair over. Essentially, they killed their victim in a way that allowed them to not have to go face-to-face with their subject. The rope symbolically allows them to distance themselves. It's not a perfect methodology, but it's a starting point. See the names above."

This cleared out the majority of the remaining students. There was only five of us left on the stage. This surprised me. I assumed most people had chosen the gun. I guess to assume that meant I assumed most people thought like me. Turns out that wasn't the case.

"Finally," Ronald said, "we have our five that used the gun. This kind of killer when given the option takes the middle ground. Not too barbaric with their kill, but not too soft either. They're efficient and empathetic. They kill with emotion and purpose. They accept what they are, but don't derive joy from the act of killing. It's strictly business. They're very universal, which is why they're called the Gray Matter Elitists; because technically these individuals could fall within any division and fit right in, but we've created an accelerated group for these people instead."

My name flashed up on the Jumbotron and I stood to
join my new peers under the gold banner.

Chapter 3

Ronald concluded his speech, and the orientation for that matter, with a few inspiring quotes and tidbits of advice on being successful in the program. Then we met with our division leaders in the auditorium to begin a tour of the grounds.

The division leader for G.M.E. was a tall slender woman. She looked like a runner because of the lean muscle built around her boney arms and legs. She wore a ponytail and introduced herself as Nat. Short for Natalie.

Nat began our tour by explaining that the auditorium was used for all announcements and get togethers for the divisions. Then she led us out to the dining hall.

The dining hall was directly behind the auditorium. There was an outdoor grill, probably because weather would never be a problem underground, and an indoor dining area.

The indoor dining area looked like a high school lunchroom with the addition of a high-end bar toward the back. A bar that served more than alcohol because the community had a variety of ages. They served protein shakes, smoothies, lattes, cappuccinos. Things of that nature also. It appeared to be a very active place with people constantly milling about.

"The cafeteria and outdoor grill are free for all residents. The bar inside and all the restaurants are not. When you get to your rooms each of you will have an envelope with some 'starting out' money. Think of your schooling as your new job. You will get a weekly allowance or paycheck for your participation during studies. The better you do in your studies then the better your allowance will be. Contrary, the worse you do the less you get paid," Nat said so matter of factly.

Spread out from the dining hall both left and right were a variety of small shops. It was amazing how expansive the underground town was. It stretched for miles. One shop in particular caught my eye. It was part of a strip of stores built from red brick and had a yellow neon sign out front that read: **Killer Ink: Tattoo Parlor.** There was some art in the window of skulls that overlapped a variety of weapons, as well as other impressive artwork.

Nat skipped over the other divisions housing, since we would never step foot there, and took us to our housing.

The Gray Matter Elitists were housed on a floor beneath the city, Nat explained. Even further underground than we already were. Nat was going over the logistics of the ventilation system and how they get quality breathable air to the underground town when she led us into one of the restaurants.

The restaurant was sports themed. There were televisions on every wall displaying a variety of sports.

Where there weren't any TV's there were posters of famous athletes like Michael Jordan, Muhammad Ali, Lionel Messi, and many more.

Toward the back was a full-fledged bar with more liquor on the wall behind the counter than I'd seen in my entire life. In the far corner of the room sat a phonebooth. Some sort of prop that didn't really fit with the theme. Nonetheless, it made me smile because it reminded me of Superman. As fast as the flash of happiness came it left just as quickly as I thought of my parents and how much I missed them.

Nat told us to have a seat and that dinner was on the house for our first meal. Until I was sitting down and staring at the menu, I didn't realize how hungry I was.

The five of us G.M.E. newcomers and Nat sat at the same table which gave me the opportunity to meet my peers.

There was a scrawny middle-aged man named Hank who had glasses pushed snug against his face in a way that made him look intelligent. He was scouted like the rest of us and brought to the community, so he probably was as smart as he appeared. It definitely didn't seem like he was recruited for his physical capabilities. Unlike Nat's lean arms, his weren't coated with muscle.

There was a thicker woman who looked to be in her twenties. She introduced herself as Terry. She was pretty excited about the sports theme the restaurant had, claiming to be a boxer herself. I figured that was probably her ticket into the program.

A teenage boy a couple of years older than me introduced himself as Curtis. Curtis had broad shoulders and no neck. He was short and reminded me of a block. He appeared to have stunted growth from years spent in the gym. He was someone I pictured using the rope to kill his test subject, yet here we were. What did I know?

Then there was Karlie. She was the first to ask about my scars. Surprising myself, I felt comfortable telling the group about my condition. They all agreed it would be a huge asset in a place like the community, where we were being trained to be assassins. Karlie even remarked, "An assassin who feels no pain? That's awesome."

Karlie was on the skinny side, but thick where it counted. Her personality seemed to be all bark, but I had a feeling that her bite was just as bad. She was plastered with tattoos. More ink showed than skin and for some reason that made me more attracted to her. She was roughly my age with bleached blonde hair that had one purple strand falling close to her face.

"You should get those scars covered up with some ink," Karlie suggested a ways into our meal.

I was working my way through some hot wings when she said this and I responded very impolitely with a mouth full of food, "I thaw a pwace… here that does…" I took a swig of Coke. "Tattoos." The lack of manners was so unlike me, but so was killing a person not that long ago and now look at me. I wasn't quite sure who I was anymore.

"Scars hurt like hell to get tatted over, but I guess since you don't feel pain that won't be a problem for you. We should go tonight," she said.

Not thinking, I stuffed another wing into my mouth before I could respond, so I just nodded. Not fully realizing what I was committing to.

We finished off our meals and the light-headedness that was creeping in from malnutrition faded away. On top of that, I was slowly starting to accept my reality. I was even somewhat eager to see our living quarters.

Nat led us out of the restaurant and I immediately felt a sense of disappointment. Because Nat explained our living quarters were a ground floor beneath us, I thought for sure there would be some insanely cool entrance and I had strong suspicions that entrance was the telephone booth in the corner.

We rounded the corner of the restaurant and walked through an alley, not too dissimilar to the one I'd killed Woody in. The similarities caused a rush of emotions to flood my brain to a point where I felt as though I might topple over and cry but finding inner strength I tucked the whirlwind of emotions away to deal with another time.

Nat escorted us to a pair of dumpsters toward the back of the alley. They were a dark green that made them barely visible in the shadows.

She stopped us just before the dumpster on the left and pulled something out of her pocket to pass around. Hank was the closest to her, so he took one and passed the rest around the circle we'd formed.

It was a solid black, thin rubber bracelet that had a red blinking light the size of the tip of a needle. If we weren't in the dark, we probably wouldn't have been able to see it blinking.

Once everyone had one on their wrist Nat said, "This is your access to all things G.M.E." She nodded to Hank, "Place the bracelet where the light is blinking flat on the lock."

Hank grabbed the fancy looking padlock on the dumpster and touched his bracelet to it. There was a quiet click and the padlock unlocked.

As Nat opened the lid a hidden set of stairs unfolded in front of the dumpster. We used those stairs to climb into the dumpster. Only the inside of the dumpster wasn't a dumpster at all. It was a deep elevator that went down to our new living quarters.

Our living quarters were set up like a college dorm. We each were assigned our own room and there were private bathrooms down the hall.

My room was a little bit smaller than my old one at home. There was a queen-sized bed on the far wall and opposite of that was a closet with doors that stood next to a desk and a small sink next to that.

On the desk was an envelope, a bathroom kit, and keys to the room. I opened the envelope and found some cash as well as a note:

Welcome to the Skilled Individuals' Community. We're excited to have you as part of the team. Here's some starting out money and you'll find clothes in the closet. Best of luck in your studies.

I walked over to the closet to see if there really were clothes and sure enough the closet was full.

I felt like a shower, but as I was preparing to leave there was a soft knock on the door, so I opted for a quick wash of my hands and face in the sink before going to answer it.

I opened it slowly, a little unsure of who to expect on the other end.

"You ready to go?" It was Karlie.

"Go where?" I asked. Although, I had a feeling I already knew.

"You committed to getting tattoos with me tonight, remember? And don't tell me you don't have any money because I already opened my envelope and there's plenty in there to spare. You also can't tell me you're scared because you don't feel pain, so… let's go."

There was no arguing with her logic. At least not a reason I could think of, so I grabbed my keys, the money, closed and locked my new bedroom door, and followed after her.

As she walked, I started to notice what her tattoos actually were. She was wearing a tank top that showed off her colorful, skinny arms. She had a theme that carried over on both arms. A surprising theme for tattoos. All of her tattoos were Disney characters. She had Mickey and Minnie. Donald Duck. The Lion King. Beauty and the Beast. Cinderella. Pretty much the whole gang in all sorts of bright colors that went well with her purple strand of hair. She was as intriguing to me as she was beautiful.

Chapter 4

I'd never really pondered the idea of getting a tattoo. I wasn't necessarily against it. I'd just never considered it, but now that it had been determined I'd be getting one I started thinking about what I should get. I was even starting to stress a little bit. There were so many possibilities to choose from.

Inside Killer Ink: Tattoo Parlor, there was loud music playing overhead. It was Denzel Curry; a rapper Mason had shown me. The memory saddened me momentarily, but then a soft hum of buzzing needles became audible beyond the music and brought me back to the present.

Karlie grabbed my hand and led me over to a counter that was covered in portfolio folders of the various artists' work.

"Start looking," she said. "See if anything catches your eye."

I picked up one of the folders and skimmed over the pages. The artist's name, printed on the front, was Rex. No last name.

Combing over Rex's work it became evident that his forte was realism, but I was more into the old school, the American traditional style which meant Rex wasn't my guy.

I picked up another folder for an artist named -- I assumed nicknamed -- Cutter. Cutter's specialty was American traditional. Looking over her work, I knew I'd found my gal. All that was left to do now was figure out what I wanted to get tattooed.

After ten minutes of sifting through her art I found what I wanted. A small mousey girl met us at the counter, "You figure out what you want to get and the artist you'd prefer?"

I nodded and told her I'd like to work with Cutter. She said okay and went to find her.

From the backroom walked out a pretty redhead with a face angel marked with freckles. She stuck out her hand to introduce herself and as she did so I noticed small scars running horizontal up her arm and now understood why she was nicknamed Cutter.

Positioned upright on a chair with my arm stretched out over an armrest I watched as Cutter's needle pierced my skin and left a tiny puddle of ink behind. Cutter wiped away the ink and repeated the process until she was done, which took her well into the morning.

In one sitting I'd covered my scar riddled arms in tattoos. Two full sleeves. I went with a Sailor Jerry theme and covered my wrists to my shoulders with images of skulls, old school roses, ships, anchors, and other random American traditional images. I even put some meaningful stuff like a boar and a traditional looking bear in memory of my adventures with my best friend, Mason. One of the traditional roses had my mother's name in it and I did a traditional lion with my father's name blended into the mane.

To finish up the sleeve, Cutter let Karlie tattoo a solid black rose. She did pretty good for not being an artist and being exhausted from sitting with me all night. This shared experience made me feel for her. She was a beautiful girl and I caught myself imagining a future with her as I watched her laugh with Cutter about how crazy it was I now had two sleeves. Two sleeves tattooed on me in one night. That was crazy and so was the thought of two assassins, who were really just kids, having a life together.

Even though I couldn't feel pain, I could feel fatigue and it weighed on me heavily. Karlie was tired as well. As we walked, she grabbed my arm and laid her head on my shoulder.

"Thanks for letting me take you to get tattooed. Can't believe you decided to cover ALL your scars. Looks good though," she said.

I found comfort in her strawberry scented hair resting nicely on my shoulder and said, "Thank you. That was fun. I like being tattooed better than I like being covered in scars."

As we climbed into the dumpster, I held her hand to help her down into what was actually the elevator to our living quarters. In the elevator she didn't press the down button. Instead, she leaned in and kissed me. Not just a peck, but a full-on intimate kiss that I gladly eased into. Her lips were warm and tasted like mint. After a minute or so of kissing she pressed the down button and we made our way back to our own rooms saying nothing except goodnight.

In my room I smiled at the thought of the whole experience, then I climbed into bed and slept like a baby.

It wasn't even three hours after closing my eyes to sleep that I heard a quick rattling knock on my door.

Still groggy and not thinking, I answered the door in my boxer briefs. It was Nat.

"Put some clothes on and join the rest of us," she said.

"Where are we going?" I demanded.

"You'll see," she said and started walking away with the group following behind her.

I snagged a T-shirt and some pants and ran after them, not wanting to get left behind and forced to find my way in our underground maze.

Nat took the group to the elevator in the dumpster, but instead of going up to the main street, we went down a floor. To do so she had to scan her bracelet. I don't think ours would have worked because when we scanned ours last night it took us to the floor our rooms were on. We didn't have the option to go lower.

The floor below our living quarters looked like a lab for testing. For testing what I didn't know, but the sight of it unnerved me a little. I started speculating what we were doing here. Nat said nothing as she led each of us to a separate room.

The room I was in had a hospital bed with leather straps. Nat told me to make myself comfortable and that someone would be joining me shortly. I sat on the bed feeling uncomfortable about the straps. Me being uncomfortable about the straps made me wonder what the others, who could actually feel pain, thought.

Two minutes later a plumper gentleman walked in. He was balding on top but made up for it with a burly beard. He didn't bother introducing himself and I didn't bother asking. What I did ask was, "Why am I here?"

What I meant was what are we doing in this room, but he took that to mean what was I doing in the community, in this program.

He gave a very sophisticated answer, "Well, son. You were selected. Scouted out by one of our recruiters. It's no accident you're here. Once they find a candidate in our data base that sounds promising they do extensive research on them and if they continue to find interest then they find a way to come into contact with the candidate. There's more planning than you could possibly imagine. They dive so far into your psyche that they even claim they know what weapon you're going to use in the passage before you do. Nine times out of ten they're right. They had over a ninety percent correct prediction rate with this round's recruits. On the surface this place seems simple but trust me boy… it's not. There's a lot that goes into finding subjects like yourself and more complexities still. More than I even know myself. Now, are you ready?"

Was this true? Did Ms. Bristol know she was recruiting me even before she met me? Did my name show up in their data base of potential recruits? As all these thoughts passed through my head the plump man pushed over a machine, which brought my attention back to the present.

"What's that?" I asked.

The machine was a small box that the man opened like a waffle maker, but instead of the squares that held syrup this machine had a handprint inside.

"This is a fingerprint remover. You place your hand in this. I'll close the lid and the mold will adjust to the size of your hand. Once I press this button on top a liquid will fill the tips of the mold, an acidic blend created right here in these labs, and then you'll no longer have traceable fingerprints. It's extremely painful, but your chart said you feel no pain so this should be a cakewalk for you," the man said nonchalantly.

I feared more for the others than myself. Specifically, Karlie.

As if reading my thoughts, the man said, "Don't worry, your friends who do feel pain will be heavily sedated.

Matter of fact their anesthesia should be kicking in right about now, so let's begin so we can get you out of here at the same time."

I placed my right hand in the mold and waited for about ten minutes until the man said, "Alright, next hand."

After another ten minutes with my left hand this time, I no longer had fingerprints.

The man led me out of the room stating, "This acidic blend only burns away what it needs to, so the healing process is only a couple of days but until it's healed all the way don't pick at the thin layer of scabbing you'll see."

Out in the hall I met back up with Nat and the other G.M.E. members. Karlie looked sleepy. She smiled sheepishly at me and joined my side.

"I imagine I'm going to feel this tomorrow," she said examining the tips of her fingers. "And I bet it'll hurt way worse than a tattoo, but hey, at least the lingering effects of the medicine are nice. I'd imagine this is how you feel all the time. Lucky."

Was I lucky though? I always thought God gave humans pain for a reason, a warning system to danger. I wasn't lucky in my mind. In my mind my inability to feel pain was simply a flaw in one of God's creations.

Nat took us back to our rooms and suggested we get some rest to allow the anesthesia to wear off. She said she'd be back later in the afternoon to take us to our first class.

I was tired, but it wasn't from an anesthesia, since I had none. It was from my night out with Karlie getting tattooed. I was surprised no one said anything about my new ink. No one probably cared. We were all still getting our feet wet. Trying to make sense of it all. I did notice Nat shaking her head as she scanned over the traditional theme though. So at least someone noticed, even if it was disapprovingly.

I desperately wanted to climb back into the unmade bed but could smell a slightly sweet and slightly sour body odor coming off me and decided I better shower first.

Feeling clean and refreshed I closed my eyes. Moments later I drifted off, dreaming of Karlie's tattoo covered arm reaching out for me. Hand in hand, she led me to another quiet spot in the community where we shared another kiss. That's what I dreamed anyway. Who knows if such a thing would ever happen again?

More dreams about the community and the new people I'd met here joined Karlie in my head. Dreams of new replacing memories of old.

<u>**Chapter 5**</u>

The afternoon came quicker than I'd imagined. It felt as if my door was being knocked on the moment my head hit the pillow, not hours later.

It was Nat and the whole G.M.E. group, and I was extremely satisfied to see that I wasn't the only one who looked groggy.

We boarded a unique subway and were taken to the D.M.P. part of town. Our first class took place in a large glass structure, my guess was that it was some sort of greenhouse. It had an intense lighting system to warm the plants and was chock-full of a variety of greenery that had a mist of water raining down on it.

"Don't touch any of the plants," Nat warned. Considering we were in the Division of Many Poisons; I took Nat's warning very seriously.

We were led along a red stone path to a row of stone benches in an open grassy area within the glass structure. I assumed we'd be joining the other D.M.P. members, but not seeing any of them around I guess that wasn't going to be the case.

A woman who looked to be in her late forties early fifties with long vibrant red-orange hair strolled in from the opposite end of the greenhouse to address our group. She had a dark green business suit on and square framed glasses.

This couldn't be serious? I chuckled to myself. This woman was like a modern-day Poison Ivy pulled straight from the Batman comic books. I glanced around at my peers to see if any of them were as amused at this woman's appearance as I was. None seemed to be. The look had to be intentional.

"Welcome to the art of poisoning," the modern-day Poison Ivy said. "My name is Penelope Vargas and I'll be your instructor for the next few weeks."

* * *

The art of poisoning with Penelope Vargas was a fire hose of information that we were expected to soak up like sponges. We, unfortunately, were promised an exam at the end of her teachings that we'd be expected to pass in order to move on to the next segment.

Penelope had a very hand on teaching style. For one of the lessons she spent the morning lecturing us on common poisonous flowers and their effects on humans. Then to make the lesson hit home she put three flowers in front of each of us. The Foxglove, which if consumed would cause a severe headache, stomach pain, and possibly fainting. The Wisteria flower which can cause stomach pain also, along with diarrhea, and vomiting. The third flower was the Borage flower which caused no sort of pain and had a nice cooling taste.

She didn't show us any images during her lecture but if we were paying enough attention to what she was saying then we'd be able to easily identify each flower.

"Choose a flower to eat," she directed the class. Or in other words, select your poison.

I wouldn't feel a headache if I accidently chose the Foxglove, but I definitely didn't want to be crapping my pants, so I did my best to avoid choosing the Wisteria flower. I recalled Penelope describing the Borage as a blue, star shaped flower with furry leaves. I selected my flower and scarfed it down. Right away getting the cool taste she'd mentioned and knowing I'd chosen correctly.

That night at dinner you could tell who chose what flower as we sat at the same sports theme restaurant we all met at.

Karlie ate the Borage, the same flower I did. She was in an upbeat mood, smiling, and flirtatious.

Terry was bored during the lecture portion and ended up eating the Wisteria flower, which sent her sprinting to the bathroom every twenty minutes, gripping her stomach. She didn't eat much at dinner and left early.

Hank was scarfing down a pepperoni pizza and looked to be feeling pretty good, so I'm assuming he ate the same flower as Karlie and I.

Curtis gripped his head and moaned. He chugged glass after glass of ice-cold water, so I'm guessing he accidently went with the Foxglove. This would be a lesson for him and Terry to do better for the final exam.

When exam day came, I was unable to sleep, so I woke up early and started my morning with one of my 'off season' workouts. Something my old coach prompted us to do to maintain our shape and form throughout the year while we weren't playing.

The workout began with a light jog, then some circuit stuff (push-ups, sit-ups, etc.), and always ended with an all-out sprint that left me gasping for air.

After I'd cleaned up, by taking a nice shower and putting on some clean clothes, I went and knocked on Karlie's door.

"Come in, doors unlocked," she shouted from within.

I found Karlie pacing her bedroom, nibbling relentlessly at her fingernail.

"You nervous?" I asked. Dumb question. Of course she was. She was practically chewing off her finger.

She stopped and looked up at me, "I don't like exams and I don't know what to expect today, so yeah Luke, I'm nervous."

I nodded, if I was being honest with myself, I was nervous too, "Well why don't we take our minds off the exams for now and go get some breakfast?"

"Good idea," she said and was out the door before I could offer a response.

Karlie and I had grown to love the small restaurants expanding throughout the underground town, way more than we enjoyed the cafeteria. Unfortunately, that meant we had to pay for most of our food, but we did well enough in our classes that our pay was enough to cover our habit of being foodies.

For breakfast we went to a diner called Simply Syrup. The first thing I noticed when we entered the place was the wall filled with all kinds of syrup. They had strawberry flavored syrup. Blueberry. Citrus. Caramel. You name it. They even had a shelf with varying degrees of sweetness for maple syrup.

Their menu had four items on it: waffles, pancakes, French toast, or eggs (served any way you like). At the bottom of the menu was a list of all their syrups. There were over a hundred different flavors.

I ordered waffles with a vanilla flavored syrup. Karlie ordered scrambled eggs with extra cheese of all things.

"Not interested in trying any of these crazy flavored syrups?" I asked with a smile.

"Not today, I just want to get something in my stomach. I'm too nervous about the final exam," Karlie said with not even a hint of a smile on her face.

I devoured the sweet tasting, vanilla waffles, because at that particular moment I wasn't nervous about the exam. I could eat without any problems. Karlie on the other hand, got two bites in before running to the restroom to bring those two bites, and whatever other liquids lay in her belly, right back up.

Karlie and I stayed together while the minutes ticked away, inching us ever closer to our exam. We strolled the city streets, finding new little nooks where she allowed me to steal a few more kisses. Only because it helped get her mind off of the final today. I didn't care what her reasons were. I enjoyed kissing her. I hoped the exam never came. I wanted to milk every second of this day together. She was a beautiful distraction from the thoughts and memories of my old life.

When the exam finally arrived, Nat led our group into a building on the complete opposite side of the greenhouse where we'd taken our advanced course in various poisons.

"This is the Testing Center," Nat explained to all of our confused faces. "All finals will be held here."

Penelope strolled in as Nat finished up, she was wearing a dark purple suit today, and the two of them separated each recruit into a private room in the basement floor of the building.

The room had a desk with a chair in the middle. On the desk were two rose colored boxes. They had a strong resemblance to a jewelry box my mother had on her dresser. The memory pained my heart for a moment, but that's all I would allow; a moment. No sense dwelling on the past, when the trajectory of my future relied upon which box I chose.

There was a note, and a steaming cup of water with a spoon protruding from the top, between the boxes. The note read:

In front of you lies two boxes with a description of what's inside written on the front. Choose one and make yourself a nice cup of tea. When the tea is finished, you'll know if you passed or not. As always… we'll be watching.

I read the description on the box to the left first:

Like my neighbor I am white, my shape umbrella like, and our resemblance is uncanny. With a narrow eye find our difference at the stem and leaves. I am hairless and blotched with purple. Who am I?

I thought I had an idea of the flower inside, remembering back to one of our lessons with Penelope, but I read the second box to make sure:

As you know, I am white and umbrella like. My name has royalty. However, if my name doesn't give it away then maybe the hairs on my leaves and stem will. Who am I?

I now knew which flower I was going to choose, 'my name has royalty' solidified my decision. We had a very specific lesson on Umbels, flowers that had an umbrella like shape and the two flowers that were discussed in depth that day were the Queen Anne's Lace, Daucus Carota, and Poison Hemlock, Conium Maculatum. One extremely poisonous and the other completely edible. A life or death decision. A fifty-fifty chance.

I opened the box on the right and pulled out, what I believed was Queen Anne's Lace. Knowing I was being observed I mixed the flower in the water with confidence, even gave it a minute to steep before chugging it. Then I waited…

I focused on my breathing, waiting for my breaths to shorten as life was squeezed out of me. Waited for my vision to blacken, to send me into eternal darkness. I waited for any indication that I'd chosen wrong. That I'd failed. But no such indicators came. I was fine.

Moments later, an animated voice echoed throughout the room. Penelope's voice, "Congratulations, Lucas. You passed."

Chapter 6

There was a small foyer outside the testing rooms. When I entered the foyer, Hank was already there waiting. With his glasses pushed high up his nose and a cheesy grin on his face, he said, "Lucas, glad you made it. I watched them wheel a body bag out of Curtis's room. He wasn't so lucky."

"Then why are you smiling?" I asked, confused at his enthusiasm.

"Well, because I made it."

Wow, I thought to myself before replying, "If this was the first class imagine what they'll make us do in the next ones." That took the smile off his face.

A few minutes later Terry strolled out. She looked sweaty. I would venture that she completely guessed at which flower to drink in her tea.

"Phew," she muttered.

I stared at Karlie's door. I knew she was stressed but she was smarter than Terry and Curtis. I didn't have an ounce of worry that she'd make the right choice. Not until minutes had passed with no sign of her.

"Nat said we don't have to wait, right? That we could go when we were finished?" Terry asked, looking like she wanted to get out of the Testing Center to shred the blanket of anxiety she'd been wearing.

"Want to grab a bite?" Hank asked her. "You look like you could benefit from a decent sub."

Without any consideration for Karlie they left. Meanwhile, I stared at the door as if I could open it with my mind and pull Karlie from the struggles within.

Minutes turned to an hour. Now I was worried. I paced the foyer. Where was she?

Slowly the handle to the room moved. I held my breath, relieved and eager to wrap my arms around Karlie as she emerged.

The door opened, but it wasn't Karlie that stepped out. It was a large man pushing a gurney. On that gurney was a black bag. A body bag.

Like a wicked witch splashed with water in the movies, I melted to the floor. Collapsed on top of myself. Karlie was dead, and I couldn't control the heavy sobs as they took control of my body.

* * *

Our hybrid group of five assassins in training was now down to three. My whole life I'd been numb to pain, but for the first time I felt a new kind of pain that I had to become numb to.

My heart weighed heavy at the loss of Karlie. Only knowing how to move forward, I stomached the newfound pain and put all my efforts into the program.

Into becoming the hard, cold blooded killer they wanted me to be.

Our next course I blew through with ease because of my experience with hunting. It was the Long-Distance Killers' course that was taught by a man who had snake eyes. Literally, slits for eyes like a reptile. It was obvious that they were contacts, but paired with his shredded military-built body, it was nonetheless intimidating.

The man's name was Martin Hammer, I wondered if his birth certificate read that same name or if it was one, he adapted as his military life started to form. He told us to call him by his nickname, one all of us predicted with ease, Snake.

Snake was a highly regarded sniper for a secret unit of the U.S. military. A unit disclosed to very few. Those few being in very high places. Apparently, the nickname was given to him because of the way he moved through the grass; military crawling so fast his comrades thought he resembled a snake slithering.

The final exam for the L.D.K. course also took place in the Testing Center.

For this final exam we weren't placed in a room. Instead, the remaining members of G.M.E. were led to a large area that had rows sectioned off by metal dividers. Each row was assigned a number. There were at least fifteen rows. I was placed in row seven. The two other members, Terry and Hank, were separated at least five rows away from me on each side. At the end of each row was a cage, with something indiscernible inside.

We were each given a small rope, like the one in the bag on the day of the passage, and a rifle with a single bullet. Snake made our instructions clear, "You have one shot to kill the animal that comes for you out of that cage. Should you miss, your only saving grace is your rope. And good luck with that."

The three remaining members of G.M.E. shared a moment of anxiety at the unknown. Wondering what could be in those cages.

I couldn't help but smile as Snake counted down from five and the cage door was opened. It was just like being back home with Mason in the forest when that boar came charging toward me.

I lifted my rifle and on the exhale of my breath buried a bullet in between the mad creature's eyes. It happened so quickly there wasn't even a squeal. Not from my target anyway. There was a squeal, however, to my left and I could hear Terry screaming as she wrestled with the boar in her row. She must have been trying to wrap the rope around its neck with no success.

To my right I heard a gunshot and the sound of an animal slowly dying. Apparently, Hank's shot wasn't as clean as mine, but it got the job done. Leaving two members for the final course.

Chapter 7

For the weeks following the L.D.K. exam I stayed in my room as much as I could. Only venturing out to eat and only eating for necessity, not pleasure. This meant a lot of free meals in the general cafeteria, where I'd often see Hank intermingling with a variety people from the different divisions. Trying to impress them with the fact that he was one of two remaining members of the accelerated G.M.E. group.

I thought differently, I saw us for what we were; sacrificial lambs. A group of individuals skilled enough to be chosen to serve our country, but people who no longer existed on the public record. In other words, we were expendable. Every single one of us. Handpicked by a complex algorithm and close scrutiny from a recruiter, but told we ended up where we were because of choices we made; choosing to join the program, choosing our weapon to decide our division, choosing to kill, choosing to continue in the program. The program was designed to make us feel like we had a choice, but I knew the truth now. We never had a choice; we were just tricked into believing we did. Pawns in a much bigger game.

I was angry that I was the government's tool, angry for being another number to them, but the anger that weighed the heaviest was because of Karlie's death. All this anger I stored deep inside myself and used it to excel in the program.

Our last class was the Division of Physical Abilities. This final course was taught by a short, boulder of a man named Brent Hunt, another name I was suspicious of. Was it given at birth or acquired later in life? Brent looked like an Olympic sprinter.

For six weeks we ran through military techniques for hand-to-hand combat, using weapons and devices I'd never even heard of. Brent's favorite was the combat knife. He loved a good knife fight.

I was under the impression I was doing extremely well; it wasn't until I saw my reflection in the mirror that I noticed how many deep cuts and surface bruises I'd received from the fighting. I looked like a stereotypical prison inmate, tatted and scarred from head-to-toe.

The final came rapidly, and I found myself once again back in the Testing Center.

For this exam we were back in the small rooms, except this time there was nothing in the room except a wall full of weapons.

Brent advised each of us to choose one weapon for the fight. He said based on the weapon we chose he'd pair us with one of the permanent D.P.A. members for a fight to the death.

I scanned the wall, looking for my weapon. There were so many options: spears, axes, hatchets, war hammers, maces, clubs, daggers, knives, billhooks, falxes, and ones I didn't remember going over in class.

I kept it simple and pulled a hatchet off the wall. As I did so the wall flipped in on itself and the weapons disappeared, leaving me in an empty room holding a hatchet.

"Now that you've chosen your weapon the fight will begin. I'll count down from five and your opponent will enter. Five… four… three… two… one…" Brent Hunt's voice faded away and the door opposite of me opened. Slowly, my opponent walked in. The first thing I noticed was his smile, like a kid at Christmas time; his white teeth shining like snow against the night. I gulped down a nervous bubble in my throat as my eyes fell upon the war hammer he was swinging eagerly. We'd met before.

Devin charged without any warning and wind milled the hammer at my face. I side stepped and launched myself in the opposite direction of where my foot landed. The hammer slammed against the concrete floor and released an earache of a sound.

Devin was swift and spun with the hammer in a crafty side swing, going for another strike. This time he connected with my shoulder. I couldn't feel it but I knew he'd done some damage.

Luckily, it was my left shoulder and I'd chosen a weapon I could use with one hand.

We now stood opposite of one another as Devin smiled and prepared for his third and final strike.

I prepared myself for another blow. My left arm was now just extra weight and useless to me.

Devin raised the hammer and yelled like a madman running into a battle.

I raised my axe and hucked it as hard as I could at Devin's head. It missed and caught him in the neck.

A crimson liquid colored the floor, indicating I'd won. I'd made it through the S.I.C. program.

<u>Epilogue</u>

There was a ceremony for my completion of the program. It was small and intimate, few people came. I was allowed to phone my parents and let them know I'd graduated from the Skilled Individuals Community program and that I was now entering a career as a government worker. Ms. Bristol made it clear that I needed to be vague. That the only objective of the call was to let them know I was okay, that I was now entering a good career as a government employee and they didn't need to worry about me.

It'd been a few weeks since I was done with the program. I continued to train in the underground community and was awarded better housing. I now lived in a two-bedroom apartment with my own bathroom and kitchen. I even had a television, but it didn't get used much.

I had just finished slapping together a ham and cheese sandwich and cracked open a can of Coke when there was a single knock at my door.

I took a quick swig of the Coke, swishing it around to savor the flavor, then walked over and answered.

It was Ms. Bristol. She was wearing a tight red dress and had her hair pulled back, all but one strand. She was stunning. In her hand she held a manila envelope. And next to her stood my best friend, Mason Mills.

I was speechless as I struggled to put two and two together.

Ms. Bristol stole the silence, "Mason here has successfully passed our IT program. With flying colors, I might add. Therefore, I am assigning him to be your eyes and ears for your first assignment. You two will make a good team."

"We already do," I said with a grin and a hug for my best friend.

She handed me the manila folder, stamped with a red 'confidential' and added, "Good luck."

THE END.

About the Author

Josh Petersen is a family man that lives in Ogden, Utah with his wife, 3 yr. old boy, and Pocket Beagle. His passion is storytelling, and writing happens to be a great way to tell stories. He sincerely hopes you have enjoyed this tale he has crafted for you and that you look for more of his work.

www.ingramcontent.com/pod-product-compliance
Lightning Source LLC
Chambersburg PA
CBHW021213130726
47988CB00002B/642